Clint leaned against a post just outside the Whitecap and watched what happened across the street. Mostly, he kept his eye on the kid to see how he would react to the men who were just about to get his attention.

If the kid was surprised, that meant he obviously wasn't expecting them.

If the kid was scared, he might take off running and give the gunmen a good laugh.

If the kid was stupid, he might just get himself killed.

The last possibility didn't set too well with Clint, but it was definitely something he had to keep in mind. Just to be on the safe side, Clint stepped over to another post so he could lean against it and watch the other side of the street from a better angle.

The kid definitely looked surprised as he turned at the sound of approaching footsteps. The wide-eyed expression on his face would have brought a smirk to Clint's if not for the glint of panic in the kid's eyes. That glint showed more than fear.

To the other two gunmen, that glint was like raw meat dangling in front of them.

Clint didn't have to wait long to see the kid do something stupid. The moment he saw Henry pull his shirt up to reveal the gun stuck under his belt, Clint was bolting across the street like a shot . . .

THE GUNSMITH

309

OUTLAW'S RECKONING

J. R. ROBERTS

JOVE BOOKS, NEW YORK

THE BERKLEY PUBLISHING GROUP
Published by the Penguin Group
Penguin Group (USA) Inc.
375 Hudson Street, New York, New York 10014, USA
Penguin Group (Canada), 90 Eglinton Avenue East, Suite 700, Toronto, Ontario M4P 2Y3, Canada
(a division of Pearson Penguin Canada Inc.)
Penguin Books Ltd., 80 Strand, London WC2R 0RL, England
Penguin Group Ireland, 25 St. Stephen's Green, Dublin 2, Ireland (a division of Penguin Books Ltd.)
Penguin Group (Australia), 250 Camberwell Road, Camberwell, Victoria 3124, Australia
(a division of Pearson Australia Group Pty. Ltd.)
Penguin Books India Pvt. Ltd., 11 Community Centre, Panchsheel Park, New Delhi—110 017, India
Penguin Group (NZ), 67 Apollo Drive, Rosedale, North Shore 0745, Auckland, New Zealand
(a division of Pearson New Zealand Ltd.)
Penguin Books (South Africa) (Pty.) Ltd., 24 Sturdee Avenue, Rosebank, Johannesburg 2196,
South Africa

Penguin Books Ltd., Registered Offices: 80 Strand, London WC2R 0RL, England

This is a work of fiction. Names, characters, places, and incidents either are the product of the author's imagination or are used fictitiously, and any resemblance to actual persons, living or dead, business establishments, events, or locales is entirely coincidental.

OUTLAW'S RECKONING
A Jove Book / published by arrangement with the author

PRINTING HISTORY
Jove edition / September 2007

ISBN: 978-0-515-14353-9

JOVE®
Jove Books are published by The Berkley Publishing Group,
a division of Penguin Group (USA) Inc.,
375 Hudson Street, New York, New York 10014.
JOVE is a registered trademark of Penguin Group (USA) Inc.
The "J" design is a trademark belonging to Penguin Group (USA) Inc.

PRINTED IN THE UNITED STATES OF AMERICA

10 9 8 7 6 5 4 3 2 1

ONE

A man with a fiddle started to play a waltz from his stool in the corner of the Whitecap Saloon. Although his playing was fairly good, his efforts weren't appreciated by the saloon's customers. As soon as the gentle tunes drifted from the fiddle player's instrument, he was met by a hearty round of boos and grunted profanities.

The fiddle player winced after he realized he truly wouldn't be able to play his song all the way through, and he reluctantly launched into a halfhearted rendition of "Camptown Races." Much to his dismay, the fiddle player heard several grateful claps.

While that good-natured applause continued, the front door of the saloon was pulled open to reveal a young man standing outside. His light hair was tousled and his face was dirty thanks to the stiff breeze whipping through the town's streets. He had the look of the wild in him, which didn't catch many of the drinkers off their guard. The town of Birdie's Pass was a stone's throw from the mountains, after all, and many of the men who lived in Montana had a much wilder look in their eyes.

Once the drunks in the saloon got a look at the boy still standing in the doorway, they shifted on their feet and got back to their own business. The bartender took a bit more

interest, however, and raised his voice after a few more
seconds.

"Hey!" the bartender shouted.

That caused the young man to jump a bit and grab the
edge of the door. He did his best to regain his composure
by puffing out his chest and forcing a scowl onto his
smooth face.

"In or out, boy!" the bartender shouted. "Folks come
here to get out of that damn wind, not have it blowin' dirt
into their drinks!"

Faltering a bit in his efforts to look mean, the boy took
one step forward and paused. He let out a breath, dragged
his other leg along into the saloon and then pushed the door
shut. When the thick wood smacked against the frame, the
boy flinched.

The barkeep studied the kid for another second and then
turned to nod in another direction. After that, he got back
to his bottles and glasses as if the boy no longer existed.

Glancing around, the boy ground his teeth and studied
the mix of humanity leaning against the bar or hunched
over one of the tables. Since nobody seemed to be looking
at him any longer, he allowed the scowl on his face to drift
away.

"Hello there, stranger," a soft, gentle voice said from
the boy's right.

When he turned to get a look at who'd crept up on him,
the boy reflexively slapped his hand against a bulge under
his shirt on his right hip. Fear filled his eyes, which was
quickly replaced by embarrassment when he saw who'd
spoken to him.

The woman was in her late twenties and had short blond
hair that was cut to just shorter than shoulder length. Her
cheeks were full and her eyes were smiling every bit as
much as her thin, red lips. Curls of hair drooped into her
eyes, which she swept away with the back of her left hand.
Offering her other hand to the boy, she said, "My name's
Shelly. What's yours?"

Glancing down at the hand she was offering, the boy reluctantly took his own hand from the bulge on his hip. "Henry," he told her. "My name's Henry."

"That's a good name for a handsome fellow like yourself," she replied while taking his hand in a warm grip and shaking it. "What brings you to the Whitecap, Henry?"

"I . . . uhh . . . I'm looking for someone."

She smiled knowingly while letting go of Henry's hand and running her fingers up along his arm. Shelly didn't stop until her fingers were slowly tracing a line along his back. Leaning in closer to him, she whispered, "Think you might be looking for me, Henry?"

Henry's eyes widened, and he turned to look at her directly in the eyes for the first time since she'd sidled up to him. His eyes were wide and clear as a pond. Although he looked to be in his mid-teens at first, the longer he drank in the sight of Shelly's body, the more years were shaved off of him.

Finally, Henry swallowed hard and softly replied, "I don't think so, ma'am."

Turning her head a bit and giving him a stern look, Shelly replied, "No need to call me ma'am. You make me feel like I'm teaching you your alphabet." When she didn't get a response from Henry, she asked, "How old are you?"

The decision of whether or not he should lie flitted across Henry's face like a moth dancing too close to a lantern. Actually, it was a bit more obvious than that. Realizing that he wasn't about to fool much of anyone, Henry replied, "Thirteen. I'll be fourteen in the winter."

Shelly patted his shoulder and nodded approvingly. "Fourteen's a good age. A young man can learn a lot at that age." As her hand drifted along his body, she allowed it to stray toward the bulge under his shirt. Henry flinched dramatically, so she pulled her hand back.

Almost immediately, her hand started moving to another bulge in Henry's clothes. This one, however, was a bit farther south. Shelly lowered her voice to a soothing whisper and leaned in close enough for Henry to be able to smell the lavender oil she'd put into her most recent bath.

"You here for a taste of whiskey?" she asked.

Although Henry's eyes were on the bar, he shook his head. "No."

"Don't tell me you want to play cards. You'd be better off giving that money to me instead of handing it over to those cheats."

Henry looked toward the card games, and his eyes narrowed to focus intently upon what was happening there.

By now Shelly had guided Henry over to the end of the bar that was closest to the door. Since it was the section of the saloon that caught most of the light thanks to the dirty front window, it was also the section where the fewest of its customers could be found. Positioning herself next to Henry, but between the boy and the more populated section of the bar, she leaned against the wooden structure and licked her lips while moving her eyes up and down the boy's frame.

Henry looked at her and instinctually glanced at the slope of her cleavage, which was displayed in the plunging neckline of her blouse. Pulling his eyes to her face, Henry said, "Maybe there is something you could do."

Nodding, she said, "Go on, Henry. I'm listening."

"It's . . . kind of hard for me to say."

"I know, sweetie," Shelly replied as she reached out to run a hand along the boy's shoulder. When she found his shoulder and upper arm, she grinned and added, "You're a strong young man. Where'd you get such big, thick muscles?"

"Workin' on my pa's ranch."

"I bet you're the strongest hand he's got."

Henry's eyes narrowed as he shifted more toward the bar. He leaned on his elbows and glared at the chipped wooden surface.

Trading a quick grin with the bartender, Shelly rubbed Henry's back and leaned in so she could whisper her next question directly into the boy's ear.

"You want to be with me, Henry?"

Henry didn't shake his head. He didn't even move.

"If it's your first time, that's all right," she told him. "I'll be real gentle. You just say the word and I'll take you to my room and we can have a real good time."

"I don't want to go to your room," Henry said sternly. Quickly looking over at her, he flushed in the cheeks and lowered his eyes. "I do, but that's not why I came."

"Then why'd you bring all that money, Henry?" Shelly asked.

The boy flinched when he heard that and quickly dropped his hand to the smaller bulge in his pants pocket. Shelly's hand was already there, and she didn't move it away even after she'd been discovered. Instead, she eased her hand away from the bulge and let her fingers wander elsewhere.

"I know you've got a good amount of money in your pocket," she whispered. "It's more than enough to cover what I'd charge. You'd have enough left over to go around again. If you're feeling randy, I might just let you have a free one so you could try your hand at cards or have that drink. You might need a touch of whiskey when I get through with you."

Henry straightened up and pulled away from her. "That's not what I came here for."

Without losing her calm, Shelly asked, "I thought you said you were looking for someone."

"I am. I'm looking to hire a killer."

TWO

Clint had seen the boy walk into the saloon. In fact, Clint had been one of the only ones apart from the bartender who'd taken much more than a passing notice of the kid. Once he saw Shelly walk up to him and start working her magic, Clint had grinned and wished the kid the best. Any boy could do a hell of a lot worse than have someone like Shelly break him in.

The cards had been warming up, but not enough for Clint to recoup his losses. One bad thing about a hole of a place like the Whitecap Saloon was that it lowered a man's expectations where the gambling was concerned. With no real stakes being wagered, no familiar gamblers' faces about and only dregs tossing their money onto the tables, the odds of finding a challenging game were slim to none. Unfortunately, even the dumbest drunk could get lucky.

Clint fanned his cards and looked down at the four, five, six and seven of diamonds, with the king of spades tossed in for good measure. After a round of bets, he threw out his king and prayed to get one of the cards needed to make a winning hand. There were plenty of possibilities. In fact, Clint was even feeling optimistic when he took the replacement card that was flipped his way and fit it into his hand.

That enthusiasm ran dry, however, the moment he saw the king of hearts staring back at him.

A slender hand slid onto Clint's shoulder just then, followed by a sultry voice drifting toward his ear.

"Mind if I pull you away for a second?"

Clint didn't have to look back to know who was talking to him. "Sure, Shelly. Anything for a lady."

With that, Clint gratefully tossed his cards away and stood up from his spot at the table. A few of the other players looked disappointed, but the next round of betting was more than enough to draw their attention back to the game.

"Hope I didn't interrupt anything," Shelly said.

Clint laughed and gathered up the few chips of his that remained. "You might as well say the same thing to a horse with a broken leg before shooting it. What's on your mind?"

Shelly's entire manner had changed since she'd walked from the bar to the table where Clint had been playing. Now she strutted through the Whitecap with her hands on her hips and her chin held high. Her clothes may have been frayed at the edges, but she wore them like a queen wore her royal gown.

"You see that kid over there?" Shelly asked.

Clint looked to where she was pointing and nodded. "Yeah. I saw him when he walked in." It took a moment for Clint to spot the kid again, simply because of the difference in height between Henry and the rest of the men at the bar. "Is he causing some trouble?"

"Not at all. In fact, I'm worried about him getting into trouble."

"That's what a kid his age is supposed to do in a saloon," Clint replied with a chuckle. "That's how we learn."

"He's not in here for that sort of thing. I already checked on that." Glancing nervously between Clint and Henry, she added, "He's in here to hire a gunman."

That caught Clint off balance and he looked over to the kid one more time. "Are you sure about that?"

Shelly nodded. "He's even got enough money with him to do the job."

"Why would he want to do something like that?"

"I don't know. He wouldn't tell me. I barely got him to say that much before he brushed me off and headed on to do his business."

"If a boy that age could brush you off when you're looking as good as you are," Clint said, "he must have the weight of the world on his shoulders. Either that, or he's just not seeing straight."

Shelly smacked Clint's shoulder just hard enough to get his attention. "This is serious, Clint."

Mumbling a few halfhearted grunts as he rubbed the spot where Shelly had hit him, Clint turned and looked around the saloon. "I don't even see where he went."

Shelly turned on the balls of her feet and made the same turn to glance in all directions. Finally, she stopped and pointed toward the back of the room. "He's right over there and he's talking to some men that he's got no business talking to."

Clint looked over there and spotted the kid without much delay. Henry was having a conversation with some men with dirty faces and guns on their hips, but nothing much was coming of it. "Looks like those fellas are about to push him toward the door. That'll scare him out of here for a while."

"You're acting like this is a joke."

"The boy's not in any danger," Clint explained. "I walked into my first saloon when I was younger than him and got thrown out not long after. If someone goes and tells him to leave, he'll probably just look at it like a dare to come back later. So long as nobody gets hurt, there's no problem."

"That's just it. I'm afraid he'll get hurt."

Clint looked at her and immediately recognized the seriousness in her eyes. "Do you know that kid or something?" he asked.

"No, but I've seen others pulling the tricks you're talking about. Believe me, a woman in my line of work is usually a young man's first stop when he screws up the courage to walk into this place. That kid over there wasn't like one of those others. He's not here to drink or play cards and he's not here to get under my skirts. He told me he was here to hire a gunman and I believe him."

"You're serious?"

Shelly nodded. "Serious as hell and I'd bet that kid is even more so."

"All right. I'll go over and see what I can do." Clint looked over to where Henry had been standing and found the spot to be empty. The rough fellows who'd been talking to the kid were glaring toward the front door, so Clint followed that line of sight to find Henry walking out with his head hung low.

"Looks like the problem's already solved," Clint said. When he saw the gunmen stalking toward the door in Henry's wake, he added, "Or it just might have gotten worse."

THREE

When Clint spotted the kid on the other side of the street, he could tell that Henry had no clue what was walking up behind him. Clint could barely make out a side of the kid's face and one arm, since the two armed men from the Whitecap Saloon were standing in the way. Those other two walked steadily toward Henry like dogs stalking their prey.

Rather than rush across the street and force anyone's hand, Clint stayed in front of the Whitecap and waited to see what would happen. For all he knew, the other two gunmen were continuing whatever conversation they'd been having.

Henry could very well have asked the men to step outside for one reason or another.

As long as things remained on this same track, Clint wasn't too anxious to stick his nose in where it didn't belong. After all, experience was still the best way for a kid to learn how to handle himself when he stepped through the gate of his parents' house.

Clint leaned against a post just outside the Whitecap and watched what happened across the street. Mostly, he kept his eye on the kid to see how he would react to the men that were just about to get his attention.

If the kid was surprised, that meant he obviously wasn't expecting them.

If the kid was scared, he might take off running and give the gunmen a good laugh.

If the kid was stupid, he might just get himself killed.

That last possibility didn't set too well with Clint, but it was definitely something he had to keep in mind. Just to be on the safe side, Clint stepped over to another post so he could lean against it and watch the other side of the street from a better angle.

The kid definitely looked surprised as he turned at the sound of approaching footsteps. The wide-eyed expression on his face would have brought a smirk to Clint's if not for the glint of panic in the kid's eyes. That glint showed more than fear.

To the other two gunmen, that glint was like raw meat dangling in front of them.

Clint didn't have to wait long to see the kid do something stupid. The moment he saw Henry pull his shirt up to reveal the gun stuck under his belt, Clint was bolting across the street like a shot.

"That ain't scaring nobody, kid," the first gunman said. "So you might as well pull yer shirt back down and hand over that wad of cash yer carryin'."

Both of the gunmen looked to be more than double the kid's age. They wore clothes that were tattered and held together by the stains soaked through the material, and both of them reeked of the liquor they'd been drinking. The first one had a barrel chest and a long beard that was filled with bits and pieces from a week of suppers. The second gunman was a bit younger and a whole lot thinner than the first, displaying a broken set of yellowed teeth in a slack-jawed, vaguely oblivious expression.

Henry's eyes darted back and forth between both of the gunmen as his hand wavered in front of the pistol stuck under his waistband. "If you don't get away . . . I . . . I swear I'll . . ."

"You'll do just what the man said," Clint announced as

he stepped behind the gunmen and planted his boots in his spot.

Instinctively, both gunmen hopped to one side and turned so they could look at Henry and Clint with a minimum of fuss. That put both gunmen facing each other in between the other two. They hadn't pulled their own weapons from the battered leather holsters around their waists just yet. At first, they didn't look as if they needed to. Now they knew better than to make an overly hasty move.

Clint nodded in appreciation of the gunmen's restraint. "Might as well take a breath and walk away, you two. Surely this boy ain't worth all this fuss."

"You'd think twice about that if you saw the cash he's carrying," the second gunman said. "There's enough for all three of us to split and be on our way before someone steals my spot from the bar."

Henry listened to that and pressed himself against the front of the saloon that was across the street from the Whitecap. Even though the door was a few steps away, he didn't seem able to move his feet enough to get him there. Instead, he kept backing himself up until he was flattened against the side of the building.

Turning toward Henry, the first gunman lowered his head and stepped forward. "Hand over that money, boy, and be quick about it."

"You . . . you said you wouldn't do the job."

"I'm doin' all I need to get that money right now. If it don't work, I can always take it from yer pockets after I beat you to death."

Despite the fact that he looked as if he was going to crawl up the side of the building in order to get away from those gunmen, Henry swallowed and said, "You do the job and I'll pay you."

The first gunman stopped and glanced over at the second. Both men looked at each other silently for a moment before breaking out into laughter. "You hear that?" the first gunman said. When he glanced over his shoulder, he found

Clint standing behind him and watching what was taking place. "That kid's got some balls, I'll tell you that."

"Balls, but no brains," the second gunman added. He reached to a scabbard at his belt, pulled out a rusty hunting knife and said, "Maybe I'll cut his balls off and toss 'em to a dog."

Henry began to tremble as sweat trickled down his face.

Clint moved forward to pull the man with the knife away, but spotted movement from Henry before he could get there.

The kid made the worst move possible when he reached for the gun tucked under his belt.

Seeing what the kid intended to do, Clint spat out, "Don't do that!"

Henry didn't listen.

FOUR

The kid drew his gun in a surprisingly fluid motion. Because he hadn't been drinking for several hours beforehand, Henry appeared to be much more skillful than the other two gunmen in front of him. Those two men made up for their lack of sobriety in plain viciousness as they both took steps to kill Henry for the money in his pockets.

The man with the knife lunged forward like a snake and almost escaped Clint's grasp. With a little extra effort on his part, Clint grabbed hold of his shoulder and spun him around before that man could swing his blade at Henry.

Rather than draw his modified Colt, Clint balled up his right fist and delivered a sharp jab directly into the gut of the man with the knife. His knuckles drove deep into the man's stomach, pushing most of the air from his lungs in the process. Somehow, though, the man kept hold of his knife while also staying on his feet.

Clint's eyes were on the first gunman as he delivered a quick knee to the man in his grasp. He felt an impact with what he thought was that man's head, but tossed him to one side before checking to make sure. After that, Clint lowered his shoulder and threw himself into the man who was now drawing his pistol to fire at Henry.

The gunman caught Clint's shoulder in the small of his

back. Letting out a pained wheeze, he was tossed to one side while also tightening his finger around his trigger. The gun went off in the gunman's hand with a roar that swallowed up Henry's surprised scream.

Henry watched what was happening with confusion and fear etched onto his face. He'd drawn his gun, but hadn't even gotten his finger on the trigger yet. That changed when he saw the man with the knife rushing straight toward him.

As Clint wrestled with the first gunman, he heard another shot fired. It was a different sound than the first shot, which told Clint that it had come from another weapon. Clint took a quick look behind him to see if Henry was still standing.

Not only was the kid still on his feet, but the man with the knife was reeling backward and clutching his side.

Clint knew better than to turn his back on the first gunman for one more second. Whipping around to face him, Clint saw the man closest to him grit his teeth and raise his gun to take a shot at him. Watching those movements were more than enough for Clint to know just how sluggish that man was. Rather than draw and fire his Colt, Clint snapped his gun hand out to snatch the pistol from the gunman and send it flying at the man with the knife.

The flying gun caught the other man in the forehead with a jarring crack and dropped him into an unconscious heap.

Clint turned to face the other gunman once more, while drawing his Colt in a smooth motion. All Clint had to do from there was scowl at the gunman as if he was one second away from pulling his trigger.

The gunman's hands shot up into the air and he immediately stumbled backward. "All right, all right," he shouted. "Take the money. It's yours."

"If I see you pulling anything like this again, I'll drop you where you stand," Clint warned.

"Fine! Just don't kill me."

"If I hear about you looking at this boy again, I'll find you."

The gunman didn't even have enough left in him to speak. He just nodded and kept backing away.

"Get the hell out of my sight," Clint said.

Running as if the devil was nipping at his heels, the gunman took off and rounded the nearest corner to leave his friend laying in the dirt.

Clint holstered the Colt and looked down at the unconscious man. The knife was still in the man's hand. There was a fresh wound just below his left armpit, but it wasn't much more than a deep scratch.

Henry was looking down at the man on the ground. His gun was still in his hand and shook just as much as the rest of him. "Is he . . . ? Did I . . . ?"

"He's still alive," Clint said. "You didn't kill anyone." Walking up to the kid, Clint reached out and took the gun from him. As much as he wanted to crack the kid upside the head with the pistol, Clint took a deep breath instead. "But if you didn't want to take the chance of killing someone, you shouldn't have even brought this pistol with you."

Still staring down at the unconscious man, Henry nodded.

Clint grabbed Henry by the front of his shirt and shoved him back against the building. He didn't knock the kid very hard against the wall, but he sure as hell got the kid's attention. "Are you listening to me? You could have killed someone with that gun! You most likely would have gotten yourself killed."

There was still fear on the kid's face, but he choked it down and did his best to meet Clint's eyes. "I can handle myself," he sputtered.

"Yeah, you did a real fine job here!"

Clint stared the boy down until Henry looked away. By that time, Clint's blood was cooling off and the tension from the scuffle was fading away. Letting out a breath, Clint loosened his grip on Henry's shirt and took a step back.

"Are you all right?" Clint asked.

Henry wasn't able to maintain his defiant glare, so he averted his eyes and nodded. "Yeah, I'm fine. What about him, though?"

Looking down at the man on the ground, Clint replied, "He's fine, too. Your shot just grazed him."

"You sure?"

"Yep. His bleeding's already stopped. He'll be in some pain, but he'll be able to walk back into that saloon once he wakes up. You want to stand here and wait for that to happen?"

"No," Henry said quietly.

"All right, then. Where do you live?"

"I can get home on my own."

Clint let out a laugh and held up his hands in surrender. "Fine by me. I just thought you might like some backup in case this fellow wakes up or if his friend circles around to catch up with you."

Sure enough, those words sparked a fearful glint in Henry's eyes. Clint fanned that spark into a flame as he turned his back on the kid and started walking as if he was more than happy to wash his hands of him. After the count of four, Clint heard Henry's voice drift through the air.

"You really think that man'll come back?"

Clint stopped and turned around. Not only had the kid allowed one more second than Clint had guessed before stopping him, but Henry also managed to keep his chin up and his chest out.

"He may or may not come back," Clint said earnestly. "It'd be wiser to be ready for the first choice than be surprised by the second, though."

Nodding as if everything that had passed was his idea, Henry said, "I could use some backup." His eyes brightened as he added, "And I could repay you for helping me out."

"What'd you have in mind?"

"I can buy you a drink."

The smile on Clint's face came more from genuine surprise than anything else. "Buy me a drink?"

"To thank you. One man to another. It's the least I could do."

Clint started walking back toward the Whitecap. "Sounds good. Let's go."

A good chunk of the bravado that Henry had displayed left him when he looked at that saloon. "Actually, I was thinking about another place."

"This one'll do. If you're going to act like a man, you can face up to your actions." With that, Clint walked toward the front door of the Whitecap Saloon.

Although Henry wasn't happy about following him, he was even less happy with the prospect of staying on the street by himself.

FIVE

When Clint walked into the Whitecap, only a few of the men inside looked his way. When Henry stepped through that same door, however, he got plenty of lingering glances.

Some of those glances were from armed men who looked at the boy with the same intent that had been displayed by the two gunmen outside. A few looked surprised to see the kid up and walking, and at least one face looked relieved.

Shelly rushed forward and took the boy's face in her hands. "Are you all right?" she asked quickly.

Henry's first impulse was to grin from ear to ear at the sudden show of affection. "I'm just fine. A little scraped up, but I'll survive."

Clint rolled his eyes and said, "The kid's a regular quick draw. Actually, I believe his feet were a little quicker."

While Henry didn't appreciate Clint's comment, Shelly barely even noticed it.

"I'm just glad you're alive," she said.

After Shelly finished fussing over him, Henry took a few moments to collect himself before he was ready to say anything to her. By the time he was ready, he found her back was already to him and she'd moved on to other things.

"What happened out there, Clint?" Shelly asked. "I heard shooting."

Clint shook his head and signaled for the bartender. "Just a few panicked shots, is all. No harm done."

"Better not be any harm done," the bartender said. "Them two are some good customers."

Clint locked eyes with the man behind the bar and said, "Don't worry. They'll be back to drink your whiskey soon enough. Maybe they'll get a discount for trying to rob a kid outside your own place without you lifting a finger against it?"

"I didn't know what they were up to!"

"Is that so?"

Although the bartender was ready to come to his own defense, he faltered under the brunt of Clint's accusing stare. He looked away and grunted, "Serves the kid right for flashing so much money around here."

Clint ordered a beer, which was quickly set in front of him. After that, the bartender found some more pressing matters to attend to at the other end of the saloon.

"The man's got a point, you know," Clint said. "What were your plans for all that money?"

The kid lowered his eyes, folded his arms and rested his elbows against the bar. Before too long, he felt a pinch at his ear as he was dragged upward once more.

"Answer him, Henry," Shelly said as she pulled roughly on the kid's ear. "What were you . . ." She looked around suspiciously and then finished her question in a much lower voice. "What were you doing with that money?"

"I told you," Henry grunted. "I need to hire a killer."

After setting down his beer, Clint snapped his fingers and pointed toward the kid's pocket. "Let's see that money."

Henry's eyes widened as he straightened up. "You beat the hell outta them two outside! Would you work for me?"

Clint merely rubbed his forefinger against his thumb.

Digging into his pocket, Henry got the wad of money. He kept it close against his body and wrapped up in two tight fists as he asked, "Are you gonna earn it or take it from me?"

"I'd say I already earned it," Clint replied.

Henry let out a defeated breath and let his head droop forward. His eyes pinched in at the corners as he handed over the money in frustration. "Just take it," he groaned. "I can't do nothing against you."

Clint took the money from Henry's hands before it was allowed to fall onto the floor. The wad of cash disappeared much more easily within Clint's hands as he cupped them around the money, as if he was protecting a lit match from strong winds. Flipping through the bills, Clint nodded slowly.

"There's enough to hire a killer, all right," he said while handing the money back to Henry. "You probably could have hired two of the caliber you'd find in here."

As much as Henry wanted to take his money back, he didn't reach for it right away. "You're not taking it?"

Clint shook his head and was about to hand it back when he noticed a few of the drunks in the saloon paying a bit too much attention to him. Tightening his fist around the money, Clint stuffed it into his own pocket just as Henry was beginning to reach for it.

"Your first lesson today is to use your head," Clint told him. "You were almost robbed once today and you're going to be robbed again if you don't try to keep this money more to yourself. The first was a lack of experience, but there's no excuse for the second."

Still holding his hands out, Henry nodded. Once Clint's words sank in, Henry retracted his hands and glanced about nervously. Sure enough, there were plenty of dirty-faced drunks eyeing him. "I think I should get out of here."

"Now you're using your head," Clint told him. Feeling the uneasiness coming from beside him, Clint looked over to Shelly and added, "And he won't be going alone. I'll make sure the boy gets back home in one piece."

Shelly smiled and said, "That's very kind of you." Leaning forward, she gave Clint a kiss on the cheek and whispered, "Kindness does have some mighty good rewards, you know." After that, she walked away from Clint and let her fingers trace along the back of Henry's neck as she went by.

"Come on, boy," Clint said. "You stay here and you're on your own."

Despite the thoughts going through the fourteen-year-old's mind, Henry stayed close to Clint as they put the Whitecap Saloon behind them.

SIX

It was a cold night and the winds were blowing in from the nearby mountains. Although they weren't at the base of any rock walls, the mountains in Montana never seemed more than a stone's throw away. With winter on its way, the sun dropped below the horizon as if it was weighted down, and the shadows already seemed twice as thick now than the last time Clint and Henry had left the Whitecap.

Clint stepped to the street and looked over to Henry. The kid wasn't much more than a foot shorter than him, but he looked up at Clint as if he was squinting at the top of one of the nearby mountains.

"Which way do you live?" Clint finally asked.

The kid turned on his heels to the right, stuffed his hands into his pockets and started walking.

Clint followed his lead and turned the collar up on his jacket. "So your name's Henry?"

"Henry Hasselman, yes, sir."

"That's a name that rolls off the tongue."

"It's from my father."

Clint nodded and kept walking. "Where's your father?"

Henry drove his hands a bit deeper into his pockets and stared down at his feet as if he needed to silently command them to move. Even in the darkness, the sadness could be seen creeping in on the edges of the kid's face.

"How long's your father been gone?" Clint asked, unsure whether or not the condition was permanent.

After a few more steps, Henry replied, "He's been dead for years. I barely remember his face anymore."

"That's all right. I'm sure he wouldn't mind, since you've been so busy and all."

Henry looked over at Clint with a glimmer of hope in his eyes. That didn't last long, however, and was soon wiped away by a grumble from the back of his throat. "You don't know that."

Clint laughed and said, "If tonight's any indication, I'd say you've been busier than anyone ought to be."

That caused Henry to laugh a bit as well, even though he struggled to keep from doing so. From there, his steps were a bit lighter as he led the way toward the edge of town.

Looking ahead a ways, Clint saw the streets open onto wider roads. Most of those roads appeared to end after less than a quarter of a mile, with one road turning into a trail that led out of town. Situated alongside the shorter, branching roads were several houses arranged in small clusters.

There were lights in the windows and some folks on their porches. A few people ran back and forth between the houses, making the area seem like a little town of its own. A few of those people looked in Clint's direction, but were put at ease when they saw Henry walking with him.

"Are you going to tell me, Henry?" Clint asked.

"Tell you what?"

"Come to think of it, I'd like to know how you got your hands on that much money. Before that, I'd like to know why you'd want to go through so much trouble to hire a gunman. Someone around here giving you trouble?"

Henry kicked at something on the ground in front of him and muttered, "Something like that."

"Who is it?"

But the kid wasn't going to answer that question as quickly as he had the first. Henry kept his head down and his eyes focused on the road. His jaw remained set firmly in place. His hands remained jammed into his pockets.

"Whoever it was must have done something pretty bad to warrant being shot down," Clint said.

But Henry wasn't playing along. He listened to what Clint said and kept right on walking. Since he hadn't picked up his pace, there was still some hope that he didn't want to end the conversation just yet.

"I bet if you think it over," Clint said carefully, "that you might not even want to go so far to teach someone a lesson."

That caused Henry to plant his feet and stop dead in his tracks. He straightened his back and looked Clint directly in the eyes. It was the first time that both of them seemed to be on the same level. "I've thought about it plenty and I know what I want. That asshole deserves to die."

Clint held his ground without challenging the young man in front of him. "Why's that?" he asked.

"Because he shot my pa."

Narrowing his eyes to study the kid carefully, Clint wasn't able to find the first hint of a lie in Henry's eyes. There wasn't even as much anger as one might expect. Instead, there was just the quiet resignation of someone who'd been forced to live with something so long that he wasn't hurt by it so much anymore.

"Someone shot your father?" Clint asked.

Henry nodded.

"When was this?"

Shaking his head, Henry turned on the balls of his feet and continued walking toward the houses. "Years ago. I told you, I don't even remember his face anymore."

"Then how do you remember who killed him?"

Henry stopped once more so he could look over his shoulder at Clint. Some of the fire was gone and was replaced by the mix of nervousness and anxiousness that had been there since the first time Clint had laid eyes on him.

"My house is right over here," Henry said. "You can come in if you like."

"I think I'll take you up on that."

SEVEN

Just when Clint was beginning to think of Henry as someone older than his fourteen years, he saw the front door of
Henry's house fly open and his mother run outside. At first,
there wasn't a way for Clint to be certain the woman was
Henry's mother. Then, after seeing the way she looked at
the boy and grabbed hold of him as though he was still in
short pants, there wasn't anything else she could have been.

"Oh, dear Lord, I was worried about you!" the woman
said. "Where have you been? Don't ever leave like that
again! I was worried out of my mind."

Henry weathered his mother's storm with nothing more
than a prolonged roll of his eyes. He stood in his spot as
she circled him and fretted with everything from his ears to
his clothes to the tips of his fingers. He knew better than to
try and stop her, so he just kept his mouth shut and waited
for a lull.

And just when he thought he might be able to sneak
away from that house without being noticed, Clint saw the
anxious woman look in his direction. Her face was slightly
rounded, but mostly thin. Kind eyes complemented a wide
mouth that naturally curved into a warm smile. Her hair
flowed over her shoulders in a way that made it look like
water being poured over a smooth ledge.

As she spoke to Clint, her voice took on a softer quality, but there was still a good amount of caution in her tone. "Are you a friend of Henry's?" she asked.

Clint tipped his hat and said, "We just met, ma'am. My name's Clint Adams."

She shook the hand that Clint offered, but her posture was growing more uncertain by the second. In fact, he even caught her glancing through the wide-open door of the house to a shotgun hanging on the wall.

"He's a friend, Ma," Henry said. "Clint helped get me out of a fight."

Seeing the woman's eyes grow wide and panic show on her face, Clint quickly added, "It didn't turn out as bad as you might think. He got into a spot of trouble and I happened to be in the right place to get him out. No harm done."

"Sure," Henry said as he took the gun from his belt. "Tell that to the man that was shot."

Although Clint expected her to react to the sight of the gun, he didn't expect her to take it from Henry's hand as though it was a toy. "Henry Hasselman, I told you to never touch this gun! Now get inside and set the table for supper."

"But it's too late for supper."

"Exactly. You were nowhere to be found, so the food got cold. That doesn't mean you shouldn't have anything to eat." Allowing her friendly manner to return, she looked to Clint and asked, "Would you like to join us?"

Still looking at the pistol in the woman's hand, Clint nodded slowly. "I guess I could stay."

At that moment, she looked down, as if she'd just realized what she was holding. Although she looked embarrassed, she still didn't seem put off by the weapon. "This must strike you as peculiar," she said.

"You could say that."

"This used to be my husband's gun. He taught Henry to shoot with it and I can never seem to keep him away from it. Ever since his father was . . . well . . . ever since his father's been gone, I don't have the heart to get rid of that gun."

Glancing toward the house, Clint caught a few glimpses

of Henry moving around inside. "I know you don't know me, Miss . . ."

"Oh, my name is Kayleen Hasselman. Please call me Kay."

"All right, Kay. I know you don't know me, but your son was almost killed today."

Normally, Clint would do anything to avoid putting such a fright into a woman. This time, however, seeing the scared expression on her face let Clint know that some rules still applied with this woman.

"My Lord," she gasped. "I thought he was just building that up. He's gotten into trouble before, so I figured this was another of those times."

Clint shook his head. "He went into a saloon waving around a wad of money and nearly got killed by a couple of robbers."

"My God."

"Do you know where he would get that kind of money?"

Kay's eyes closed slowly and she lowered her head. Rather than lift her chin again, she began nodding slowly. "I might have an idea." Turning toward the door, she announced, "You get that table set for three and then serve up the food, Henry! You hear me?"

"Yes, Ma," the boy replied.

Looking back toward Clint, Kay walked around the house and motioned for him to follow. The house wasn't very large. In fact, it seemed only big enough to have two or possibly three small rooms within its walls. Kay led Clint to the back of the little structure and then knelt down to start scraping at a patch of dirt near the base.

Clint lowered himself to one knee and was about to offer his help when he heard Kay's hand knock against something that most definitely wasn't dirt or rock.

She moved more dirt aside and eventually cleared enough away to reveal a small tin box. Taking the box out of the hole and holding it in one hand, she opened the lid and immediately let out a shaky breath. "Oh no," she whispered.

Clint looked into the box and saw only a few small chunks of dirt rattling around inside.

"What is that, Kay?" Clint asked. "What's going on?"

Standing up, Kay grabbed hold of the box in such a tight grip that she nearly put dents into the tin. Without so much as glancing at Clint, she stomped to a small back door that was so narrow, Clint needed to sidestep through it in order to follow her.

Kay made her way straight to Henry and held the box out in a trembling hand. "What's the meaning of this?" she demanded. Before the boy could answer, she snapped, "You took this money! You took this money and that gun? What in the hell is wrong with you?"

"I just wanted to—"

"Tell me later," she interrupted. "I'm too angry to listen to it right now. Get into your room and shut the door."

"But—"

"Go!"

Even though Henry was a few inches taller than his mother and outweighed her by more than fifty pounds, he winced like a scolded pup at the biting tone in Kay's voice. Henry put down the plate he'd been holding and took off for his room. The moment the door was shut, Kay took a key from a hook on the wall, fit it into the hold beneath the handle of the door that Henry had just closed and locked the boy inside.

There wasn't any more shouting once that door was closed.

Kay pocketed the key and then shook her head before looking at Clint. "It's all I can think of to keep him here," she said. "Would you still like something to eat? I've made some shepherd's pie."

"I think I'd like an answer to my first question," Clint replied. "What the hell is going on here?"

"Let me fix you a plate and I'll tell you as much as I can. It's the least I can do considering how much trouble you've been through already."

EIGHT

"Henry's father wasn't always such a good man," Kay said as she put together a plate of food similar to the one she'd already given to Clint. "I've never wanted to lie about him to Henry, but I didn't want him to be ashamed of where he came from, either."

Clint scooped up some more of the beef and potato mix with his fork and said, "That makes sense."

Taking the key from her pocket, she unlocked Henry's door and held the plate into the next room. Clint couldn't see much through the doorway, but he could tell that the room was very small and still occupied by the fourteen-year-old. Henry took the plate and walked back inside so Kay could close the door.

Although she started to lock the door again, Kay dropped the key into her pocket instead. When she sat down at the table behind her own plate, Kay couldn't help but look at the empty spot at the table between herself and Clint. "He won't leave that room," Kay said. "Henry's never defied me directly."

"Does that include stealing money and walking into a saloon with a gun?"

"Actually, I've never told him not to do that. It sounds idiotic, I know. Do you have any children, Mr. Adams?"

"It's Clint and I've never raised a child. Still . . . I've been around enough of them to know that what you said isn't so idiotic. There's grown men who stick to worse lines of thought than that."

Kay smiled and picked at her food. Her disposition took a turn for the worse as she said, "A few months ago, I would never have believed you if you told me Henry had done something like that. I wouldn't have even believed he could pull together more than a dollar or two."

"I was wondering about that."

"We were given that money not too long ago," Kay said. "A man showed up in town and started asking around about my husband. He found his way to me and said he was one of the men who rode with my husband when he was killed."

"If you don't mind me asking . . . how did your husband die?"

Pulling in a deep breath, Kay replied, "Jed was shot by a sheriff's deputy while riding in from the Badlands. And before you ask, the answer is yes. He was on the run from the law. Like I told you, he wasn't a good man. He was a good husband, though, as well as a good father."

"Sometimes a man can pull that off," Clint admitted.

"And Jed was one of those men. When he was killed, I never heard about it until over a month after it happened. He was gone a lot and sometimes wouldn't show up again for weeks or more." Kay pulled in a breath and nibbled at her food. "After he died, the law came by to ask about money he might have hidden or if I knew where to find other men Jed worked with. Before too long, it all quieted down and it was just me and Henry.

"I raised my son . . . still raising him . . . not to be like his father. I've only passed along stories that show him in a good light. Since Jed has passed on, I figure he's paid for his sins and there's no reason Henry should have a tarnished picture of his father."

Clint reached out to pat Kay's hand. "You don't need to

explain that to me. You're doing the best you could with what you've got."

Although Clint hadn't meant anything by touching her, there was a moment where both of them could only look down at his hand on top of hers. Clint eased his hand back so he could continue eating, and Kay showed him a soothing smile.

"After all this time," she told him, "it's gotten so that I've nearly forgotten about what Jed used to do to earn the money he sent home. The law doesn't even pay me any mind and folks have stopped gossiping about stories of outlaws and such."

"Has that changed?" Clint asked, even though he could see the answer in Kay's eyes.

She looked at him and held his gaze for a few seconds before nodding. "A man came here and asked about me and Henry. He acted as though he knew us, but I've never seen him in my life. When he asked about where Jed was buried, I told him to leave. You see, sometimes someone wants to follow up on those outlaw stories and get themselves a trinket from a grave or some other morbid nonsense."

Clint had heard of that every once in a while. He didn't know it was a big problem, but he didn't exactly make it his business to look into such things, either. Considering some of the terrible things he'd seen some folks do to their fellow man, there wasn't a lot that could surprise Clint anymore.

"Did the man leave?" Clint asked.

"Yes," Kay replied. "He left. Then, Henry told me he spoke to a stranger who had some stories about his father. From the way he described that stranger, Henry was talking to the same man who'd knocked on my door.

"One night, some time later, the man came back and tried to give me some money. He said it was owed to Jed and I refused. He insisted I take it and made such a fuss that Henry came to see if he could protect me."

Smiling warmly, Kay glanced toward the closed door of

Henry's room and said, "The man had a gun and I didn't want Henry to get hurt or get the wrong impression. Honestly, I didn't really know what to do. I refused the money, but the man shoved it into my hand and left. I told Henry that the stranger was a bad man and to tell the sheriff if he ever saw him around here again.

"After that, I couldn't just take that money and buy us all new clothes. No matter how much we needed that kind of money, I couldn't go through all of that and just take the money for ourselves." Locking eyes with Clint, she told him, "I told Henry I was going to get rid of the money because it was dirty. I was certain that stranger was an outlaw and that there was blood on that money."

Tears were streaming down her cheeks now, and she tried to wipe them away before they dripped onto the table. When she spoke, Kay kept her voice low and controlled. "I've tried to raise my son properly, Mr. Adams. I've tried to teach him to be a good man through and through. His father wouldn't have wanted it any other way. But we needed that money, so I kept it. I thought Henry wouldn't know so long as I used it just a little here and there when there wasn't any other choice. Most of it was still buried in that box. But . . . I guess Henry knew the whole time. He is a smart boy, after all."

Patting her hand once more, Clint said, "He is a smart boy. He's also never forgotten about what happened to his father."

"I don't even know what really happened to him. All I know is he was shot. Everything else has become muddled over the years so I don't know why he was running or who he was with."

"None of that matters in this instance. What matters is that Henry's figured out something for himself and he's acting on it. He took that money to try and hire a gunman. Does that sound at all familiar?"

Kay thought that over for a bit. "He said something about hoping the man who killed his father got what he deserved, and I told him he'll get what's coming when he's judged by the Lord above. He hasn't said anything else since then."

"Can I have a word with Henry?" Clint asked.

She looked at him for a moment and started shaking her head. "I don't think that's a very good—"

"Just one question, then. After that, I'll be on my way so you can get back to your life."

"Say it from where you are and make it short," Kay replied with a stern tone that hadn't been there before.

"Of course."

Getting to her feet, Kay stepped toward the closed door and paused just long enough to get her hands on the gun she'd taken from Henry. Kay didn't aim the pistol at Clint, but she made certain he could see it when she nudged the door open a crack. "Henry," she said through the doorway. "Mr. Adams has a question for you."

Henry started to walk forward, but was stopped by his mother's voice.

"You'll stay in your room," she said. "Just answer from there."

"All right," Henry replied.

Clint stood up and looked at Kay until he got a nod to let him know he could proceed. "Henry, who were you going to hire those men to shoot?" When he didn't get an answer, Clint added, "Was it that stranger who came by here with that money?"

A few moments passed in silence before Henry's voice squeaked from his room.

"Yes," the boy said. "He took that money from Pa and probably killed him to get it. He should be rotting in hell."

"That's enough," Kay said as she gently closed the door.

Clint nodded. "That's more than enough, ma'am. Thanks for the supper. I'll be on my way."

Kay hesitated as an apologetic look drifted across her face. Since she couldn't find the proper words to say to him, she lowered her eyes and turned her back as Clint left through the front door.

NINE

Since Clint was staying in one of the rented rooms above the Whitecap Saloon, he went back there after he left the Hasselman place. Considering what he'd heard while he was at that little house, he would have gone back to the saloon even if he wasn't staying there. About three seconds after he stepped into the place, he was spotted.

Shelly might have been shorter than most everyone else in the room, but she didn't have any trouble working her way through the crowd and shoving aside a few drunks when she had to. By the time she got to Clint, she was nearly out of breath.

"Did that kid get back home safely?" she asked.

Clint looked at her for a moment as if he was watching her dance. An amused grin came to his face and stayed there even after she began scowling up at him.

"What's so funny?" she asked.

"Is there something between you and Henry that I should know about?" Clint asked.

Shelly waved his question off as if she was swatting a fly. "Of course not. Can't I be concerned for the poor fella?"

"Sure, but I wouldn't expect you to plow through this crowd just to ask that question."

She shrugged her shoulders, which were now exposed thanks to the blouse that was pulled down to display an ample amount of skin to attract the evening crowd. Her breasts were plump and swayed nicely every time she moved. "He came to me, Clint. I don't know. I guess I just want to make sure he doesn't get hurt because of it."

Taking the beer handed over by the bartender, Clint told her, "He didn't come for you, remember?"

Smirking mischievously, Shelly said, "He might have talked along those lines, but his eyes were telling a different story. If he didn't intend on seeing what I had to offer, he was thinking about it before too long."

"Nobody could fault the boy for that," Clint said as he placed a hand on Shelly's ample backside and gave her a squeeze. "He is only human, after all."

Shelly moved closer to Clint and practically melted into the crook of his arm. "You made sure he was safe, didn't you?"

"Yes, I did."

"How sweet."

"I'd say cautious is more the word for it."

"Why?"

Without taking the time to go into every last detail, Clint gave her a quick retelling of what had happened since the last time he and Henry had been at the Whitecap. Despite the fact that Shelly had to have known some of the details already, Clint wanted to watch her and see how she reacted to some of what he said.

What concerned him the most was the part where he mentioned the stranger that had paid the Hasselman house a visit. Shelly didn't do anything out of the ordinary, so Clint was pretty sure that she didn't have anything else to add on the subject.

Clint finished his story at the same time he finished his beer. Even though there were plenty of others around, none of them but Shelly seemed to give a damn about what Clint was saying. Shelly, on the other hand, was enthralled.

"So some outlaw came over to drop off all that money?" she asked.

"Apparently. Do you know anything about it?"

"Why would I know anything?"

Clint eyed her closely until she finally crumpled under the pressure.

"Maybe I know something," she admitted.

"Go on and tell me."

"Not here," Shelly replied while glancing around at the bar and the men gathered at or around it. "Somewhere we can talk privately."

"Nobody around here seems to give a damn about any of this," Clint said. "And something tells me that you're just bluffing to get me to yourself."

Shelly's eyes widened and she pulled in a surprised gasp. "Why, Clint Adams, what an arrogant and egotistical thing to say!"

"If I'm wrong, I'll apologize."

Leaning forward with a sly grin on her face, Shelly ran her hand along the front of Clint's shirt until she was able to play with the top two buttons. "Apologize first."

"Why? Am I wrong?"

"I'd sure like to see it," she said with a shrug.

Clint laughed and put enough money on the table to cover his first beer as well as the next. "Now I know you don't know anything. As much as I'd like to stay here and play with you, I've got things to do."

"What could be more important than playing with me?"

Hearing the promise in her voice, Clint couldn't help but let his gaze wander down the front of Shelly's dress. As if playing to every movement of his eyes, she leaned forward and shifted her weight so he could see far enough down the front of her blouse to spot the hint of pink nipples just beneath the flimsy fabric.

"I was thinking of looking around for a trace of that stranger Mrs. Hasselman was talking about," Clint said.

"And I may just be able to help you with that."

"Are you joking?"

Shelly's face became serious for a fleeting moment, which was tempered by her normal grin. "Of course I'm being serious. If you don't trust me, there's one good way to find out for sure."

Clint decided to go along with her for the time being. Of course, a big factor in making his decision was the strength in Shelly's grip as she dragged him to the narrow staircase that led up to the rooms for rent.

TEN

As for rooms built over a saloon, Clint's wasn't too bad. It had a fairly comfortable bed, a washbasin and a door with a lock that actually worked. Clint didn't bother with the lock since he wasn't planning on being in the room for long.

"All right, Shelly," he said once they were both inside the room. "Tell me what you wanted to tell me."

Grinning even wider as she walked up to him, Shelly slipped both arms around him and rubbed her breasts against Clint's chest. "You just wanna dive right in, huh? I guess I can go along with that."

Clint placed his hands on her shoulders, but only so he could move her back a little. "You know what I'm talking about. I need to get going soon."

"Where are you going to?"

"I don't think that stranger Mrs. Hasselman was talking about is just going to leave because he was asked. Usually, someone who hands off that much money wants something in return."

"You think she's in trouble?"

"I don't know yet. That's why I was going to try and catch him lurking around that house."

"Do you honestly think someone lurking around the

house is gonna step right back up to his old spot so soon after you left?"

Trying to take some of the edge from his voice, Clint said, "If you tricked me up here, just say so now before I get too bent out of shape."

"It wasn't a trick." Shelly slid her hands up so they could lock behind Clint's neck. Pulling him down while she raised herself up on her tiptoes, she seemed to be climbing up Clint's front like she would a tree. "I've seen the fellow you're talking about," she whispered.

"What?"

Shelly nodded.

"Who is he?" Clint asked. "Do you know his name?"

"I don't know his name, but I know what he looks like. I also know he's no friend of the law."

"Where can I find him?"

"He walks down the street right outside this place every night around ten. That's when I stretch my legs outside and get some fresh air before the night owls come in to roost."

Clint checked the watch in his pocket and was reaching for the door before the watch was shut again.

"Where are you going?" Shelly asked.

"I'm going to find that man before he pays another visit to that family."

"But it's not even close to ten yet."

"A head start never hurts," Clint replied.

"You can wait for hours and still get your head start. I don't know where he's staying or where he comes from. Do you really think it's a good idea to take the chance of him seeing you after you were just over there for supper?"

Even though it sounded like Shelly was grasping, Clint had to admit that she was making some sense.

"He was watching that woman and her son," Shelly continued. "Do you think he may be watching you?"

Clint locked the door and turned to face her again. "If you're lying about that ten o'clock thing . . ."

"Why would I lie?"

"I don't know, but you do go to some awfully surprising lengths to get a man into bed."

"Why is that so surprising?" she asked.

"Considering the line of work you're in, it's downright shocking."

"First of all," she told Clint while unbuttoning his shirt, "most of the men who pay me usually just want to get theirs as quick as possible and wouldn't even notice if they were fucking me or a hole in the wall. Most of the times, all I need to do is take my dress off and look at their peckers and they're almost finished."

Peeling off Clint's shirt and then sliding her hands along his chest, she went on to say, "And second, the Hasselmans have lived here a long time and I wouldn't want to see any harm come to them. We may not be on friendly terms, but they're neighbors and I don't like the thought of some stranger coming in to make them miserable."

"So you know for certain the man you're talking about is the one who gave that money to Mrs. Hasselman?"

She nodded slowly. "I saw him follow her once, which is why I kept an eye on him ever since. I started seeing him take his nightly walks, but that's all I've ever seen him do. He carries a gun and he looks like trouble. A girl in my line of work needs to know how to spot fellas like that."

Clint knew better than to argue that point. In fact, women like Shelly stayed alive by being able to sniff out the rotten apples in any pile.

"And he's always on the street at ten o'clock?" he asked.

She nodded without hesitation.

Now that she had Clint's shirt off and his belt unbuckled, Shelly slipped her blouse down to reveal her large, rounded breasts. "And third, I don't go through so much trouble to bed down any man unless he's worth the effort."

"And you think I qualify on that account?" Clint asked.

With the ease of an experienced professional, Shelly

got Clint's pants down and slipped her hand between his legs. She cupped him at first and then slowly stroked his cock until it became thick and hard in her hand.

"Oh yes," she said breathlessly. "You're plenty worth it."

ELEVEN

Once he realized that there wasn't much difference in heading out now or a little later, Clint gave himself over completely to the moment. Actually, he gave himself more over to the instincts that filled his entire body the moment he felt Shelly's bare skin pressed against him.

She may have been a short woman, but her energy more than made up for her size. Shelly nearly ripped Clint's clothes off of him as soon as he stopped talking about tracking killers in the dark and started concentrating solely upon her.

Once more, Shelly practically climbed up onto Clint. This time, though, he wasn't resisting her in any way. He reached down with both hands to cup her generous backside and hold her up as he began moving toward the bed. Every step of the way, Shelly nibbled on his ear and neck as her breaths started coming faster and faster.

When Clint felt his legs bump against the bed, he stopped walking and lowered her down. Shelly wasted no time in pulling his pants all the way down and wrapping her lips around his cock. She slid her hands up and down along Clint's legs as her head bobbed forward and back.

Clint stood at the foot of the bed and closed his eyes, savoring the way her mouth slid along his penis while her tongue flicked along the bottom of his shaft. His hands moved through her hair so he could guide her movements and slow her down before she took him too close to the edge.

Obeying his gentle command, Shelly eased back and looked up at Clint with a hungry look in her eyes. Her mouth stayed open and her chest heaved with anxious breaths.

"Take that dress off," Clint said sharply.

She smiled widely and carried out the order as quickly as she could. Her skirts came off and were tossed into the pile along with the rest of her clothes. From there, Shelly propped both feet onto the bed's splintered footboard and opened her thighs to show him her smooth, wet pussy. Her fingers slid along the glistening flesh between her legs and she reached out to him with her other hand the moment Clint leaned toward her.

He felt her hand wrap around his cock once more. This time, however, she guided him into her and let out a slow, relieved breath once he slid all the way inside. Clint stayed there for a moment to enjoy the feeling of being inside of her. That feeling only got better as he began to slowly pump his hips back and forth.

Shelly lay back on the bed and closed her eyes. Reaching up and behind her, she grabbed hold of the blanket while arching her back and letting out a quiet moan. Using her left leg, she pulled Clint in closer while thrusting her hips out a bit.

Picking up on the signals her body was sending, Clint slipped his hands beneath her and pulled her closer to the edge of the mattress. He kept his hands on her backside as he pulled her toward him while thrusting his hips forward. Their bodies met with a solid impact and Shelly raised her voice until it filled the room.

"That's it," she told him. "Harder."

Clint obliged her for a while, until he felt her start to tremble with an oncoming orgasm. He thrust in and out of her a bit more and then suddenly stopped.

When Shelly looked at him, her expression was the same as if she was being robbed at gunpoint. "What are you doing? Why'd you stop?"

"I want you to turn around," Clint said.

The first time he'd spoken to her like that was when Clint had arrived in town just over a week ago. It had been a mistake, but she'd grinned so widely at him that he immediately knew when she'd like to hear that stern voice even more.

Now was one of those times, and Shelly responded by hopping onto the bed, turning her back to Clint and settling down onto all fours. Looking over her shoulder at him, she whispered, "Is this what you wanted?"

For a few seconds, Clint let his eyes roam along the gentle curve of Shelly's back. He then let his hands roam along the rounded perfection of her backside. "That's exactly what I wanted," Clint said as he settled behind her and eased his rigid cock between her thighs.

Clint held onto her hips and buried himself inside of her. Even after he was all the way in, Clint took hold of Shelly's hair and gave it a little tug as he pushed forward just a bit more. That caused her to throw her head back and let out a gasping moan as her body tightened around him.

Keeping hold of her hair, Clint placed his other hand on her backside as he started pumping faster and faster.

Shelly rocked in time to his rhythm and even bucked against him at the right time so he was pounding into her even harder. When Clint let go of her hair, she stretched forward and clawed the blanket with her fingers as her entire body was rocked by a powerful orgasm.

Clint eased out of her and positioned her on her back. Rather than settle down beside her, he climbed on top. Her weary eyes widened when she felt his rigid erection between her legs.

"Still going?" she asked. "Now, this is why I went to all this trouble."

Clint smiled, guided himself into her and said, "I'm glad you did."

Now Clint took both of her hands in his and pressed

them against the bed. Shelly's legs opened wide to accommodate him as he started rocking back and forth on top of her. Her eyes were wide open and never strayed from him.

She watched as Clint sped up and drove into her harder as he thundered toward his climax.

By the time his orgasm pulsed through him, Clint felt almost too tired to move. Shelly wriggled her hips in just the right way and pumped them at just the right time to send a wave of pleasure through him that was almost blinding.

"And you've still got plenty of time before ten o'clock," Shelly pointed out.

Clint crawled under the blanket and said, "Really? I guess we'll have to find a way to kill another hour or so."

TWELVE

It was nine-thirty when Clint stepped out of the Whitecap Saloon and crossed the street. He'd known Shelly ever since the last time he'd ridden through this part of Montana, and she didn't have any reason to lie to him. On the contrary, the worry on her face where Henry was concerned was genuine enough, and Clint was certain she wouldn't want any harm to come to any of the Hasselmans.

Still, Clint couldn't help but feel guilty that he hadn't been scouring the town as he'd first intended. At the very least, he could have picked a spot within eyeshot of Henry's house so he could watch for anyone lurking about in the shadows.

With all the bad men he saw, Clint didn't want to let an opportunity slip by to prevent another boy turning into one. Henry was a good kid, but he had that wildness about him that was all too familiar. Clint had seen it plenty of times before in the eyes of boys who grew up to rob banks or turn their stolen guns against the law.

Clint was just about to curse himself some more for wasting time with Shelly when he saw her own prediction come to pass.

Shelly was actually leaning against a post outside the Whitecap when the stranger rounded the corner at the other end of the street. Clint was watching for anyone out there, so he picked out the other man almost instantly.

The man looked to be close to Clint's height and had a wiry build. He moved with his head down and a wide-brimmed hat pulled down to cover most of his face. But Clint didn't need to see the man's face in order to get a handle on him. Watching him move was more than enough.

Walking with strong, confident steps, the man looked like a bobcat that was ready to break into a run at any second. He kept his hands at his sides and didn't swing them with his strides, so they were always within inches of the gun holstered at his side.

As he approached the saloon, he looked over and immediately met Shelly's eyes.

For a moment, Clint thought that she'd ruined his plan before it even got started. His intention had been to keep from being seen or drawing any attention. Before he could get too worked up, however, Clint saw the man tip his hat to her and walk down the street without casting a glance in his direction.

Clint had to admire the way Shelly stood in her spot, knowing exactly where he was standing, and didn't even cast a sideways glance in his direction. After seeing the way the stranger looked at her, Clint figured the other man would have been more suspicious if she hadn't been there.

Clint waited until the stranger had gone farther down the street, then began slipping from shadow to shadow behind him. Since there weren't a lot of alleys to work with, Clint had to rely more on his own eyesight and let the stranger get a larger lead before closing in on him again. Sure enough, the other man headed toward the cluster of houses on the edge of town where Henry and his mother lived.

But the stranger didn't head directly for the Hasselman place. Instead, he began circling every other house from a big enough distance that he could see who was nearby and if anyone was in the open. When he spotted the occasional fellow out for a nighttime smoke, the stranger circled in another direction. When he caught sight of a dog sniffing toward him, the stranger turned again.

Finally, like a leaf that had settled after being tossed about by a restless breeze, the stranger picked his spot. It was a thick cluster of shadows beneath a large tree. So many branches hung down from the tree that the stranger nearly disappeared as he situated himself within them.

Clint figured he should thank Shelly for holding him back until now. Apart from the obvious benefit of spending time with her, Clint had managed to stay behind the stranger's path rather than find himself in the middle of it. If he'd done what he'd originally set out to do, Clint would most likely have been discovered when the stranger went through his painstaking efforts to scout the area. Not only would Clint have been spotted, but he probably wouldn't have seen who spotted him and the stranger would have gotten away without a trace.

As it was, Clint marked the spot where the stranger was hiding and found a spot of his own to keep an eye on the other man. There was no mistaking the fact that the stranger was watching the Hasselman house. When he saw the other man start to move in closer to one of the windows, Clint worked his way to a spot where he could pay him an unexpected visit.

Clint got close enough to hear the stranger's coat flapping in the wind. He didn't think he'd made a sound, but the stranger turned suddenly to look directly at him.

In the blink of an eye, the stranger's gun was drawn.

THIRTEEN

"What brings you out here?" Clint asked without acknowledging the fact that he was staring down the barrel of a gun.

The stranger spoke in a voice that sounded like it had been shredded by broken glass. "What the hell business is it of yours?"

Clint dropped his eyes for a second to glance at the gun in the other man's hand. That was enough for him to see it was a Schofield model that didn't see much use anymore. He could also tell by the stranger's steady hand that he was more than a little familiar with that weapon.

"Seems to me like you're spying on the woman and boy who live in that house over there," Clint said.

"And I still don't see how it's any of your concern."

"Maybe the woman doesn't appreciate being spied on. Maybe she doesn't like you knocking on her door and frightening her boy." Clint narrowed his eyes a bit and tensed the muscles in his arm. "Or maybe she doesn't like seeing the face of an outlaw trying to hunt down a dead man."

The stranger was probably a fairly decent poker player, because he didn't react too much to those words. He reacted enough, however, for Clint to know that the words had struck a chord somewhere within the stranger's head.

"I ain't hunting down nobody," he rasped. "But I don't mind starting now if there ain't no other choice."

Clint held his ground without batting an eye. "There's no cause for blood to be spilled, but you're done with this family. You can walk away, run away or be carried away. One thing I can guarantee is that you're going away. Right now."

For a second, a hint of concern passed across the stranger's face. After it was gone, the steely coldness that had been there before was back and even colder than ever. Clint spotted the subtle change just in time to know what was coming. The instant he saw the stranger's gun hand move, Clint responded in kind.

Rather than drop his own hand to pull the modified Colt from its holster, Clint snapped that hand out and up to catch the stranger's wrist. Clint's movement was just quick enough to force the stranger's hand up as he took his shot. The gun roared once and sent its round into the sky over Clint's head. After that, Clint lost his grip on the stranger's wrist and felt an impact in his gut that took the wind out of him.

Clint felt the blow land and cursed himself for allowing it to happen, with the very breath that was forced from his lungs. Even though he didn't allow himself to buckle or be hampered by the blow for more than a second, Clint still wasn't able to keep the stranger from getting away.

If he was there to simply chase the stranger off for one night, Clint would have been content to let the man go. But Clint wasn't going to be in town forever, and he intended on making it so the Hasslemans could sleep soundly for a good, long time. Because of that, Clint sucked in a breath and took off after the stranger.

The other man was quick on his feet. In the short lead he'd gotten, the stranger was far enough ahead so Clint could only see the flutter of the back of his coat. Faces poked out of windows from the nearby houses in response to the gunshot, and Clint used them to keep track of the stranger's progress. All Clint needed to do was watch where the other folks were looking before they turned toward him, and he got a rough idea of where the stranger had gone.

As he raced away from the houses as well as the rest of the town, Clint felt the ground become rougher and less even beneath his boots. Every so often, his ankle would start to turn the wrong way, but he was moving so quickly that his momentum kept him from falling on his face.

Clint bolted through a row of trees and found himself looking out at an open stretch of land. There wasn't a lot of moonlight, but there was enough for him to realize the stranger wasn't anywhere in front of him. When he turned back around, Clint saw a shadow from the trees behind him rush forward like a hawk descending upon its prey.

Before Clint could make another move, the stranger had a firm hold on the front of his shirt and was pivoting toward the trees. The stranger's arms were strong enough to pull Clint along for the ride and eventually slam him against the closest tree.

Clint felt some of his breath leave him on impact, but he'd already steeled himself based on the most recent time the wind had been knocked out of him. This time, the impact only served to light an angry fire in the bottom of his stomach.

Bringing both arms straight up and inside of the stranger's elbows, Clint snapped his arms out and knocked the man's hands to either side. From there, Clint took hold of the stranger's shoulder with his left hand and then balled up his right to deliver a solid punch to the man's gut.

Clint heard the man wheeze and hack up a few haggard breaths. Still, the stranger had enough left in him to step back and pull himself free of Clint's grasp. The stranger's hand flashed toward his belt, and Clint wasn't about to stand still long enough to find out what was in store for him next.

Although Clint had been expecting another gunshot, he heard something heavy slice through the air while he dove away from the tree. Clint spun around and saw the stranger with a knife in his hand and a vicious snarl on his face. Fortunately for Clint, the knife was embedded in the trunk of the tree.

Clint didn't waste a fraction of a second before reaching

out to try and grab the knife. The stranger wasn't about to let go. In fact, he was already pulling the blade free before Clint could get to the knife's handle. Rather than try to make a grab for it, Clint took hold of the stranger's wrist so neither one of them could take an effective swing with the weapon.

Since his options were quickly falling away, Clint wrapped his free arm around the stranger's neck and moved in behind him. Just as he felt his forearm sink in deeply against the man's windpipe, Clint felt the jarring impact of the back of the man's head as it was slammed into his face.

The stranger followed up the backward head butt by letting go of his knife and twisting around to face Clint. Bringing his knee up, the stranger threw his body forward so he could pack the biggest possible hit with what little amount of space he had. The man's knee caught Clint in the midsection, just below his ribs. Any higher and one of those ribs might have snapped. Any lower and Clint might have spent the next couple minutes puking up everything he'd eaten in the last day or two.

Seeing the victorious grin on the stranger's face was more than enough to get Clint moving again. Using every bit of strength he had left, he cocked his arm back and then straightened his back. As his upper body came up, so did his fist. When his knuckles made contact with the stranger's jaw, there was enough force behind them to snap the man's head back and send him staggering backward a few steps.

Clint didn't have much of anything left. The effects of all that running, combined with the hits he'd taken, left him barely able to stand up straight.

The stranger appeared to be in the same boat, since he hunkered down with his hands on his knees and his breaths making him sound like a steam engine on its last legs.

Neither one of them was in any shape to take off running, and they didn't seem too eager to fight.

All that remained now was for Clint to figure out what the hell to do next.

FOURTEEN

Clint's hand hovered over his holster. Even though he didn't recall the moment in which he'd dropped his Colt back into place, he knew it would be there when he needed it. He'd lived by that gun for so long that it was as vital a piece of him as his own arm. Judging by the stranger's stance and the caution in his eyes, Clint was sure the man was pretty much the same in that respect.

"Who the hell are you?" Clint asked.

The stranger didn't reply. Instead, he glared at Clint intently while waiting for one wrong move to be made.

"I know you've been watching the Hasselmans," Clint said. "I know you've been watching them every night. I also know about the money you gave to them."

Finally, something struck a nerve hard enough to elicit a response.

"None of that is your business," the stranger said. "You can just forget about that money, because it ain't yours and it never will be."

"I'm more concerned with you watching that family like a hawk."

"Why?"

"Because they deserve to live in peace."

"Do you know them?" the stranger asked.

"I know them well enough to know they should be able to rest easy in their own homes. Anyone deserves that much."

"And why would you take such an interest in them?"

"Because I'm in a position where I can help, and I couldn't just ride away knowing some vulture is lurking around here waiting to sink his claws into a widow and a kid."

The stranger eased up slightly, but the difference was almost invisible. Clint might have missed the subtle shift in the stranger's face and posture if he hadn't been watching him so closely.

"You ain't the law," the stranger said.

Clint shook his head. "Nope."

"And you ain't a friend of Jed Hasselman."

"Is he that boy's father?" Clint asked.

The stranger shifted a bit more. This time, a questioning look drifted across his face. "Yeah. He sure was."

"Then I didn't know him. Something tells me you did, though."

Bringing his eyes up to look at Clint, the stranger seemed as if he'd been caught napping. He no longer focused on Clint, but looked around at every bit of movement and every bit of noise that passed through the night. Finally, he muttered, "I knew him."

Now that his blood wasn't racing through his veins and some of the pain from those blows had subsided, Clint was seeing things in a different light. The stranger himself had eased back and was now even starting to turn away from Clint. Even so, the stranger's hand was still near his gun.

"How'd you know Mr. Hasselman?" Clint asked.

"It don't matter."

"And why were you watching his family? If you were a friend looking in on them, I doubt the lady would have been so spooked."

"She's got every right to be spooked," the stranger said. "That's why I didn't force her to talk to me any more than she had to."

"And why lurk about outside her home?"

Anger flashed in the stranger's eyes as he looked at Clint. That anger left him as he averted his eyes and lowered his head. "She wasn't supposed to know I was there."

"You must have some reason for that."

"I wanted to make sure she put that money away somewhere safe. When I gave it to her, she said she'd toss it out, but she didn't. Folks have a way of sniffing out money like that. All I wanted to do was make sure nobody came after her to get it."

"That's why you've been watching her every night?" Clint asked. "To make sure she wasn't robbed?"

When he said that, Clint didn't believe it. The words sounded like something close to a joke as they hit his ears, but the stranger wasn't laughing. His eyes were focused on a point over Clint's shoulder, and he stared at it for a good couple of seconds before replying.

"Yeah," the stranger said. "That's why."

Those three words were packed with enough earnestness to swing Clint's opinion completely around. Even though he could scarcely believe he was saying it, he told the stranger, "I think you're telling the truth."

Laughing under his breath, the stranger replied, "I don't give a damn what you think."

The stranger settled upon his haunches and then lowered himself all the way down. By the time he was sitting on the ground, he looked like a set of bellows that had been allowed to drain of air until it was less than half of what it had once been.

Clint joined him by settling onto the ground facing the stranger.

"How do you know Kay?" the stranger asked.

"I just met her over supper."

"Tonight?"

"Yeah," Clint said with a nod.

"What about the kid? Did you meet him over supper, too?"

"No. Actually, I crossed paths with him when he went into a saloon in town to try and hire a man to kill someone."

The stranger's head snapped back as if he'd been swatted on the nose. "What did you say?"

"He took that money with him and tried to buy himself a gunman."

"I'll be damned. Who's he want to kill?"

"My guess," Clint said, "is that you'd be the one on his mind."

Oddly enough, the stranger kept smiling and nodded. "I suppose that makes sense. Only problem with that is how many men saw the kid carrying all that money."

"I'd be more worried about what sort of men they were instead of how many."

"Either way," the stranger grunted, "it ain't good. Looks like I botched things up pretty bad rather than makin' them any better." He got up and dusted himself off. "Do you know who the kid talked to while wavin' that cash around?"

Clint looked up at the other man without getting up. He could draw his Colt sitting almost as well as he could while standing, so there was no need to put his aching body through the trouble of climbing to his feet. "I do know that he was already jumped by a couple of those men who meant to rob him."

"Was the kid hurt?" the stranger asked as the deadly coldness seeped back into his eyes.

"No. I made certain of it."

The stranger nodded and started to walk toward the town.

Since it didn't seem as though the stranger was about to explain himself, Clint asked, "Where do you think you're going?"

"I need to set things straight so that family don't get any more grief on account of that money." The stranger kept walking and then stopped. "Since we ain't about to kill each other, do you want to help me?"

FIFTEEN

Clint walked next to the stranger all the way back to the houses that were huddled together like travelers around a fire. They took their time in getting back, so most of the commotion they'd stirred up had died down. Most of the shades were drawn tightly over windows, and the doors were all shut. Nobody was sitting on the porches, and the area was quiet enough for Clint's footsteps to crash in his own ears.

"So do you have a name?" Clint asked. "I don't like to work with someone without even knowing his name."

The stranger kept quiet for another few steps before finally glancing over and saying, "It's Matt Fraley." He paused and watched Clint as though he was waiting for something in particular.

Sensing the tension in Matt's voice, Clint said, "I haven't heard of you, but that's not too big of a surprise considering how much you like to sneak around in the dark."

Matt laughed, but it still didn't make him look any friendlier. In fact, his scarred face and harsh features were ill suited to a smile of any sort. "Who might you be, mister?"

"Clint Adams."

Stopping instantly, Matt squared his shoulders to Clint and dropped his hand to his holstered Schofield.

Clint reacted out of pure reflex and stepped back while placing his hand on the grip of his Colt.

"I've heard of you," Matt snarled. "You're the Gunsmith."

"That's right," Clint replied.

"You're practically the law."

"I've worn a badge, but not on a regular basis."

"You wearin' one now?" Matt asked.

"Would it have mattered?"

"You're damn right it would've mattered. It's the difference between you talking to me right now and you laying dead on the ground."

"We can definitely keep talking," Clint said. "But you can only try to follow through on the other. Personally, I wouldn't recommend it."

Matt didn't make another move to draw his gun, but he also didn't take his hand away from his holster. His eyes narrowed and his muscles tensed until even the wind seemed to grind to a halt around him.

Finally, Clint said, "If I'd wanted to shoot you, I would have done it a while ago. If you know anything about me, you should know that I don't need to trick a man to drop his guard."

The muscles in Matt's jaw twitched and his nostrils flared. Then, like a passing storm, the anger and suspicion that had been there a moment ago were gone. He nodded and continued walking. "You're right. Any man could've fired on me back when we were in that scrap. Hell, the Gunsmith might even stand a chance against me in a fair fight."

Keeping his own predictions to himself, Clint said, "And if I was working with the law, I wouldn't be here on my own chasing you down when I could have had a few deputies backing me up."

Matt nodded absently.

"So where'd all that money come from?" Clint asked.

"Here and there. We socked it away over more years than I can count."

"Who did?"

"Me and the boys I used to ride with." Glancing over his shoulder, Matt added, "Jed Hasselman was one of them boys."

Clint didn't react much to that news. To some degree, he'd already put that together for himself. "The widow told me her husband was a bad man."

Grinning, Matt said, "Bad . . . but not the worst. Hell, I don't even think he would've gotten into so much trouble if it weren't for me."

"So is that what you're doing here?" Clint asked. "Looking in on the man's widow?"

Matt didn't say anything to that.

"What happened to Jed? Were you there when he was killed?" Clint stopped walking and waited to see the expression on Matt's face that was like the cold edge of a sharpened blade. He didn't have to wait long.

"Did you kill him?" Clint asked.

The question was stated without emotion or accusation. It took plenty of effort on Clint's part to keep it that way, but he must have done a good job because Matt wasn't able to keep his scowl on for very long.

"I didn't pull the trigger that day," Matt said. "But I might as well have. There's plenty of folks out there who I killed, and I'll get to them soon enough. There were plenty of men who rode with me at one time or another, but Jed was a family man. He wanted to go back to his pretty wife and see his boy, but I convinced him to do otherwise. It's because of me that he ain't here no more."

"How so?"

Matt remained quiet and looked toward the dim lights behind a few of the windows in the nearby houses. His gaze locked on one of the windows, but not the one belonging to Kay or Henry. Staring into that random pane of glass, Matt said, "It just is."

Clint had had his doubts regarding Matt's intentions. He knew nothing about the man besides what Matt had told him and what he'd figured out for himself. Still, those things were enough to convince Clint to stay at Matt's side rather than try to run him off.

"So do I need to worry about the big bad Gunsmith putting a bullet in my back?" Matt asked.

"Not yet."

Matt stared at Clint for a few seconds and then nodded as if he'd taken his own personal inventory of him. "What about later?"

"We'll have to wait and see. As long as you want to lend a hand to that widow and her son, I'm willing to do what I can."

"Good. Since the boy advertised how much money he can get, we'll have to make it known that he don't have it no more."

"And how do you propose on doing that?"

"Simple," Matt replied. "We rob them."

SIXTEEN

It was getting close to midnight when Clint and Matt returned to the cluster of houses. Although they'd been watching the homes on the edge of town for a while, most of that time was spent in hushed talks regarding what they intended on doing. In the end, Matt broke away from their spot and headed toward the house that was closest to him.

Clint had to admit he was impressed by watching Matt sneak up to the homes. Matt wasn't exactly a small man, and Clint never took his eyes off of him the entire time. Even so, Clint lost sight of Matt more than once. He even had to admit that he might have lost Matt completely if he hadn't already known where to look for him.

For a few seconds, Matt huddled beside a dark house like just another unmoving shadow. When Clint got a bit closer and waved, the shadow returned the wave and then straightened up to his full height.

Matt had his bandanna over his face as he walked straight up to the front door of the Hasselman house and kicked it open so it banged loudly against the wall. "Give me all that money!" he shouted.

The commotion immediately sparked some movement behind several other windows. Curtains were pulled back, and a few lanterns were lit here and there.

"You heard what I said!" Matt shouted. "Give me that damn money!"

Clint moved in closer to the house and watched as the glow of a lantern came on in one of the back rooms. There was plenty of movement around the other houses, but those folks were still content to stay inside and watch from where they thought they were safe.

Suddenly, Clint heard what must have been Kay's voice drifting through the air. Matt said something else to her, and they had a short, somewhat heated, conversation. The conversation ended with a piercing scream that brought Clint running toward the house. Along the way, Clint pulled his bandanna up over his face.

Clint found Matt still inside with Kay. Matt had the money in his hand and a surprised look in his eyes.

"You're early," Matt said.

Clint looked to Kay and saw that she was more surprised than anything else. He drew his Colt and stepped away from the door. "Who the hell are you?" Clint shouted.

Taking his cue, Matt bolted out the door and ran straight along a path that took him past all the other homes. After tugging the bandanna off his face, Clint stepped onto the front porch, straightened out his arm and sighted along the top of the Colt's barrel. Pulling his trigger once, Clint saw Matt stumble and then continue running.

Clint took a few more steps before breaking into a half-hearted run. All the while, he fired at Matt's back, until his target finally disappeared into a shadow. Standing out for all to see, Clint flipped open his Colt's cylinder and dumped out the spent shells so he could replace them with fresh ones.

"There were two of them!" said someone from one of the nearby houses.

Looking in that direction, Clint spotted an older lady with a kerchief tied around her hair. "Did you see where the other one went?" Clint asked.

The woman looked at Clint for a few moments and then

leaned out so she could look up and down the path that wove between the other houses. "No. He must've run in another direction."

"Did anyone see where the other man went?" Clint asked loudly.

A few neighbors shouted their responses, but they quickly began shouting back and forth to one another about what they all thought they'd seen. Clint turned back toward Kay and holstered his pistol.

"Where's Henry?" he asked.

"Still in his room. Was that man . . . ?"

"Yeah," Clint replied quickly. "Did he hurt you?"

She shook her head. "He . . . didn't lay a finger on me."

"Here," Clint said as he took Kay's hand and placed the wad of money into it. "Take this and stash it somewhere nobody will find it. Nobody, you hear? Not even Henry."

Kay's face was a mask of confusion as she shook her head in disbelief. "But that man just stole this from me. Did you catch him?"

"As far as anyone knows, the man got away with every last penny of it. That way, nobody will try to steal it for real. After Henry showed that cash around town, someone was bound to come for it. This way, they'll all think it's already gone."

She nodded as everything sank in. "So that man wasn't really captured?"

"No. He was the one to come up with this idea. Frankly, I think it's a pretty good one. But you've got to do some playacting to make certain everyone buys into it. Don't show this money to anyone. If you spend it or deposit it into a bank, do so in dribs and drabs."

Now Kay nodded with assurance. "I understand," she said while tucking the money into a pocket of her nightgown and covering it with the robe she'd thrown on. "But what if that man comes back? Should I thank him?"

"He won't come back. I'll make sure of that."

She started to ask another question, but stopped so she could lean to one side and take a look over Clint's shoulder.

At that same time, Clint heard steps pounding up toward the house.

"What's going on here?" a burly man with a large, bald head asked. "Who was doing that shooting?"

"I was robbed," Kay said sadly. "This man right here chased him off."

Clint had gotten a look at the burly man and immediately spotted the badge pinned to his chest. "I think I know where he went."

"Good. Give me a moment to round up some of my boys and we can go after him."

"Just head out toward the southeast," Clint said. "That's where I'm going and I'll signal for you. If I have to change directions, I'll fire some shots into the air to let you know where I'm at."

"Are you a lawman?"

"No, sir."

"Then stay put until I come back," the burly man said as he turned and hurried away. "I won't be long."

Clint let him go without saying another word. There were more neighbors poking their noses from their houses every second, and Clint could feel the pressure to leave weighing down on him. "I'm not waiting here," he told Kay. "I need to go. When the sheriff gets back, just tell him I headed out like I said I would."

"What are you going to do when he catches up to you?" she asked.

"Don't worry about that. Just remember what I said, all right? Put that money to good use and you should be set up for a good, long time."

Kay nodded as if her neck was growing tired. Before Clint could step through her door again, she reached out to hug him and kiss him on the cheek. "Thank you," she said urgently. "And if you see him again, tell the man thank you also. I know you couldn't have pulled this off without his help."

Not wanting to waste another second, Clint left the house and ran to the stable where Eclipse was waiting. It didn't take long for him to saddle up the Darley Arabian, but he could see the group of lawmen forming by the time he left.

Pointing his nose to the eastern trail out of town, Clint rode out and then circled around to the north once he was far enough away. Birdie's Pass was behind him once more when he heard the thunder of the lawmen's horses racing off in the wrong direction.

SEVENTEEN

In the back of Clint's mind, there was the concern that Matt would be nowhere to be found when he arrived at the spot they'd agreed upon. Clint thought about that simply because he didn't know Matt very well and the man certainly had plenty of reasons to take off and never be seen again.

Then there was another part in Clint's mind that was certain he'd meet up with Matt again. Clint couldn't quite put his finger on why he thought that way, but he did. In fact, that part of his mind was even stronger than the first one.

After tussling with those two conflicting trains of thought, Clint put them aside so he could focus on the task at hand. He knew there was only one way for him to be certain which of those two possibilities would be the one to win out. He simply had to ride ahead and see which of them took place.

Clint didn't particularly like to just wait and see, especially when dealing with someone who was such a wild card.

As Clint rode to the fork in the road that he and Matt had agreed upon as their meeting place, he was actually surprised to spot a man on horseback waiting just off to the side of the trail. Clint approached carefully and was ready to draw his Colt at a moment's notice.

Matt sat with his hands folded over the saddle horn. He had a rifle hanging from the side of his saddle, but didn't make a move for it. He didn't make a move whatsoever, even after Clint rode up to him and reined Eclipse to a stop.

"What's the matter, Adams?" Matt asked. "You look surprised to see me."

"I am."

"Why? Am I in the wrong spot?"

"You're in the right spot," Clint replied. "That's what surprises me."

Mat shifted in place and looked toward the town. "Did you bring the law with you?"

Clint waited before responding to that question. His pause was put to use in much the same way he might study someone sitting across from him at a poker game. Matt didn't seem overly anxious. He didn't squirm in his seat. He barely even made a move. He just sat by and waited to see what Clint was going to say next.

"The law's not with me," Clint said. After a moment, he added, "Now you look surprised."

"Actually, I am. I figured you for the sort who would hand me over to the law once that widow got her money back."

"If you were expecting that from me, why would you be waiting here?"

Matt shrugged and took a slow look around. "Because I ain't about to duck what's headed my way no more. If the law's gonna get me, then they're gonna get me. Fighting only prolongs the running in between."

"That's very enlightened."

"I don't know what that means, as such, but I'll take it as a compliment."

Clint couldn't help but chuckle under his breath. Out of all the things he'd been expecting, sharing a few easy jokes with the admitted outlaw wasn't one of them.

"That widow did get her money, right?" Matt asked.

"She sure did."

"And you think she'll do the right thing with it this time?"

Clint nodded. "She didn't do anything wrong the first time. Her only mistake was letting Henry know where she kept it."

Shaking his head, Matt grumbled, "Maybe it wasn't a good idea to let her keep it. All it takes is one slip and she's in for a world of trouble."

"There's more good to be done with her keeping the money than in her being without it. Besides, she seems like a smart woman. She'll do just fine."

Matt was still shaking his head as he nervously put the town behind him.

"You did a good thing back there," Clint said.

"Yeah, well I tried. I got a long ways to go before I'm done."

"In that case, do you think you could use a partner?"

Matt looked over at Clint and waited as if he expected Clint to laugh or take back his offer. When neither of those things happened, Matt shifted so he was facing forward in his saddle and flicked the reins. He didn't say a word either way when Eclipse fell into step beside him.

EIGHTEEN

Clint's first reason for wanting to go along with Matt was to make certain he didn't double back and make a try for the money he'd left behind. Then, as he settled into the easy rhythm of Eclipse's steps and the cool night air washed over his face, Clint realized the error in that assumption.

If Matt had wanted the money so badly, he wouldn't have handed it over to Kay Hasselman. The look on Kay's face, along with the question she'd started to ask back at her house, told Clint that she'd recognized something about Matt's face despite the bandanna he'd been wearing. That chipped away at what little doubt there was in Clint's mind that Matt had been the one to give her the money.

Once that fact had settled inside him, Clint was left with plenty more to think about. Fortunately, it seemed the ride in the night air had had its soothing effect on Matt as well.

"Where'd all that money come from, Matt?" Clint asked.

Matt nodded to himself and replied, "I was wondering when you'd get back around to that."

Clint kept his eyes right where they'd been when he'd asked the question and didn't bother repeating it.

After a few more seconds, Matt said, "I've collected plenty of money over the years. Damn near all of it's got blood on it."

"And you decided to give some of it back?"

"No. I decided to give all of it back."

At first, Clint thought he'd misunderstood. Then, he looked for any sign that Matt might be lying. Even though there wasn't much light, Clint could see enough of Matt's face to spot the casual expression and the calm way he held himself under scrutiny. Most guilty men couldn't pull that off so well.

"Why would you give it back?" Clint asked.

"I'd think you'd know the answer to that."

"I know how I'd answer it, but I'm not the sort who'd collect a fortune in blood money, either."

"Fair enough," Matt said with a shrug. "I been breakin' the law since before I ever knew what a law was. It came easy to me. Plenty of things came easy to me. Things like stealing, lying, cheating . . . even killing. All of it became easier the more I did it.

"My uncle was a farmer and he always taught us kids to work hard and reap the rewards. I thought work was for assholes and that I could take what I wanted. Sometimes when I look back on it, I wish someone would have been able to stop me back in those days."

Matt shifted in his saddle as sounds of shouting and thundering hooves echoed in the distance. Clint took a look back there, but didn't see anything. By this time, Matt had already lost interest.

"They're headed away from us," Matt said. "They won't even get close."

"So you rode on the wrong side of the law," Clint said. "How long did that last?"

Laughing to himself, Matt replied, "Long enough for me to pull together more money than my uncle or anyone else in my family would ever see."

"When did you decide to change your ways?"

"About a year ago, when I nearly swung from the wrong end of a noose."

"I bet that's a hell of a story," Clint said.

"Not really. I was caught dead to rights by a posse who

got the drop on me and strung me up from a tall tree. They was reading me the list of my crimes and then addressed me by name to see if I had any last words to say. The only thing was, the name they used wasn't mine."

Seeing the puzzled look on Clint's face, Matt nodded and said, "I know just how you feel. I didn't know what to make of it, either. The man leading the posse took a reward notice from his pocket, held it up to my face and nearly spit his teeth out when he saw the man in the picture wasn't me."

"Who was it?"

"The hell if I know. He looked damn close, but there was a scar or two that didn't match up. The color of the eyes was different, too. I got some whores to thank for that one, since they told whoever writes up them notices the color of this other fella's eyes."

"Women do have a long memory for that sort of thing," Clint mused.

"They sure as hell do, God bless 'em."

There were some more shouts from the direction of Birdie's Pass, which caught Clint's ear. Matt heard them as well and gave his reins a snap to speed his horse up a bit. Clint tagged along, genuinely impressed by the other man's perfectly calm demeanor.

"So the posse just let you go?" Clint asked. "I've never heard of such a thing."

"Neither have I. But they let me go, gave me an apology and even offered to buy me my fill of whiskey when I got back in town to make up for all the running they made me do. They must've been too damned embarrassed to think about why I ran from 'em or didn't try to beg my way out of it when I was caught. Whoever that other fella is, I hope he can run faster than me."

Matt grinned and looked up at the stars. "Anyway, they put me in jail for a bit on account of the chase I gave 'em and so they wouldn't look like a bunch of fools to the folks paying their salaries and then they let me go. I had a change of heart after serving that time. I had a second chance, almost like them preachers talk about. I don't know whether it was God or just some awfully good luck, but I decided not to spit in the face of it. The more I thought it over, the worse I felt about all the things I done in my life."

"So you decided to make it up?"

"I can't ever make it up, but I can try to settle a few scores here and there."

"I'd say Kay Hasselman and her son are settled for a while," Clint said.

But Matt slowly shook his head. "They got money, sure, but that boy don't have a father. That lady don't have a husband. I got that man killed and there ain't nothing I can do about it."

There really wasn't much Clint could say to that. It seemed that Matt already had a good enough handle on the situation and had followed through on trying to make up for it.

"What do you mean you got that man killed?" Clint asked.

"Jed rode with me plenty of times and I coaxed him to come along again. When we got chased off of that job, Jed fell behind and I left him there to save my own skin. That money I gave to his widow was every bit of what we stole on that job. Every last cent."

"So what's your plan?" Clint asked. "Are you going to ride around handing out money?"

"I only got so much money, but that's not what all folks need."

"Sounds like you've got an awful lot of people you need to visit. Do you even know where to find them all?"

Matt thought that over and shook his head. "Nope."

"Then who gets help and who doesn't?"

"You seem to help a lot of folks, Adams. How do you decide who the lucky ones are?"

This time, Clint took a moment to think. "You know something? I don't know. I just lend a hand wherever I can."

"I got a little more direction than that, but we seem to be on the same page."

"How much longer do you have to go before this job of yours is done?"

"It may never get done, but I'll do my best. That's all I got left to do."

NINETEEN

Matt seemed to know where the posse was going before they did. While riding alongside the other man, Clint watched behind him to see if he could spot the lawmen riding in the dark. They were easy enough to pick out simply because a few of them were carrying torches to light their way through some of the trees that Clint had sent them into with his directions to the sheriff. Even without those torches, however, any man with a set of ears could have heard the commotion coming from the posse.

By midnight, Matt had steered around to the west and eventually to the southwest. When Clint spotted the flickering lights of a few windows in the distance, he raced in front of Matt and signaled for him to stop.

"What's wrong?" Matt asked.

Clint had a tired edge in his voice as he said, "We're going in circles. Do you even have a notion of where you're headed?"

"Hey, you're the one who wanted to draw all the attention. I wanted to go in and do the fake robbery quick enough to be done before the law showed their faces."

"And you didn't think the law would be after you?" Clint asked.

"They'd be after us sooner or later after a few shots were fired."

It was hard for Clint to argue with that one, so he just waved the argument off. "Do you have any idea where you're going?"

"Of course. The town's name is Lohrens."

Clint squinted as that name rang a few bells in his head. Finally, he looked down at a sign that Eclipse was standing near and read the letters painted on it. There were only seven letters on that sign and they spelled Lohrens.

"I suppose you had this planned?" Clint asked sarcastically.

Matt nodded. "Every outlaw worth his name has a plan."

"Most known outlaws get hung."

"Only if the posse can find them," Matt replied while pointing a finger at Clint for emphasis. "Ain't it great how things work out?"

It was obvious that Matt was waking up more and more as the night dragged on. Clint, on the other hand, was about to slump in his saddle from being so tired. Since all he wanted at that moment was a bed under him, Clint snapped Eclipse's reins and rode into town.

Matt came along with him, grinning smugly the entire way.

They stopped at the first hotel they could find, rented two rooms and put the horses up in a stable across the street. Once Clint saw his bed, he didn't much care if he ever saw Matt Fraley again.

A woman knocked on Clint's door to bring up a few extra blankets. She explained something about the windows being broken or cracked and that the room would get colder as the night dragged on. Clint wasn't able to pay too much attention to her, simply because he was so damn tired. The moment she left the room, he dropped onto the bed and fell asleep.

Those extra blankets remained in a folded pile at the foot of the bed.

•   •   •

The next morning, Clint awoke at roughly the same time as the sun crested the horizon. He pulled on his boots and a clean shirt before heading outside and taking a closer look at the town. The previous night, Lohrens was just a few rows of dark buildings arranged along a couple of streets. Now that the fog had cleared from his eyes, Clint could make out more than a few other details.

The first detail he was after was where he could find a lawman. A few quick questions pointed him toward a narrow old storefront one street away that had a gold star painted on its front window. A shingle hanging next to the door read: MARSHAL LIND.

Inside, the office was sparsely furnished, but well maintained. There weren't more than a few specks of dust to be found. A slender man with short-cropped blond hair sat behind a modest desk, reading a newspaper that still smelled of fresh ink.

"Marshal Lind?" Clint asked.

Without lowering the newspaper, the man replied, "That'd be me. Can I help you with something?"

"I was wondering if you might be able to answer a question for me." Clint waited for a few seconds to see if the marshal would even look in his direction. When it became obvious that he had no intention of doing so, Clint went ahead with his question. "Have you ever heard of a man named Matt Fraley?"

"Sounds familiar."

"From where?"

The marshal paused, turned a page and replied, "Couldn't say for certain."

"Do you have any reward notices posted?"

That caused the newspaper to come down. Marshal Lind glared at Clint with no small amount of distrust in his eyes. "You a bounty hunter?"

"No." Although Clint had more he could have said, he held back to see if it was necessary.

It wasn't.

"They're tacked to the wall by the coat rack," Lind said as he lifted his paper and shook out some of the creases.

Clint headed for the coat rack and found a small bundle of papers hanging from a long nail protruding from the wall. The papers slid right off, and Clint flipped through them one at a time. There weren't many of them, so Clint was able to get to the back of the pile before too long. When he flipped to the last notice of the bunch, Clint found himself looking at a fairly accurate drawing of Matt Fraley.

TWENTY

It had obviously been a few years since that drawing was completely accurate, but the younger man in the picture was most definitely the same one Clint had ridden into town with. The biggest difference between the two versions of Matt's face was in the eyes.

In the picture, Matt's eyes were cold and sharp like a blade that had been stuck into a block of ice. The eyes Clint had seen the night before were more weary and weathered.

"You find something?" Lind asked.

Clint shook his head while glancing at the rest of that notice. "Nope."

According to the notice, Matt Fraley was wanted on several counts of robbery and for killing a man in Santa Fe. The price on his head was five thousand dollars and was being offered whether Matt was marched into a lawman's custody or if he was hauled there inside a pine box.

"How old is this one?" Clint asked casually.

The marshal seemed reluctant to look away from his newspaper yet again, but he did so in order to squint at the notice Clint showed him. "That's been here awhile." He said. "I'd say at least five or six years. Maybe more since it ain't even valid no more."

Clint took a closer look at the notice and saw that the marshal was correct. A notice scribbled across the bottom marked the reward as forfeit. Clint hadn't seen that too many times, but knew it sometimes happened when whoever was offering a bounty no longer thought the outlaw was worth the price.

"Have you been working this town long?"

"Sure."

"Do you recall who this is?" Clint asked, trying to keep his frustration from his voice.

"Can't say as I do. Is he a friend of that fella you were asking about before?"

Clint didn't bother answering. Instead, he placed the notices back onto the wall. He figured the marshal wouldn't bother checking to find out there was one less than there had been before.

When he got back to the hotel, Clint found a pretty brunette sitting behind the front desk. The moment she spotted him, the brunette put down the papers she'd been straightening and showed Clint a wide, friendly smile.

"Were you too cold last night?" she asked.

"Pardon me?"

Laughing quickly, she shifted her feet and said, "I brought you those blankets, but had to leave soon after. I hope you were warm enough and didn't need anything else."

"Oh, I was fine. Thanks. Do you know if the man in room number eight is still here?"

"He's right in there," she replied, pointing to a doorway to Clint's right. "Breakfast is just being served and you're welcome to help yourself."

"All right." Clint started walking to the doorway, but was stopped when the brunette quickly spoke up again.

"If you need anything else," she said, "just ask for me. My name's Laura."

Just then, Clint realized how pretty Laura's face was. Perhaps that was because she was smiling so widely at him that she was practically beaming. The cut of her dress was

modest, but the curves of her trim body were plain enough
to see.

"Thanks, Laura," Clint said. "I'll keep that in mind."

She nodded, confident that her point had gotten across,
and settled back in behind her paperwork.

Clint stepped into the next room and immediately spotted Matt sitting at one of eight tables. A few of the other tables were occupied, but the only real movement in the
room came from a pair of servers who bustled back and
forth between the tables and the kitchen.

Sitting down at Matt's table, Clint slapped the notice he'd
taken from Marshal Lind's wall and asked, "Look familiar?"

"Well, good morning to you, too," Matt said.

"And to you. Now answer my question."

"You should try some coffee. It sounds like you could
use a cup."

When Matt saw that he'd failed to get Clint's expression
to change, he looked down at the yellowed paper under
Clint's hand. "I haven't seen that one in a while."

"That's a pretty healthy sum they're offering for your
scalp."

Matt nodded. "One of the higher ones, too."

"Maybe you should tell me why I shouldn't hand you
over to the marshal."

Scooping up some of the scrambled eggs from his plate,
Matt shook his head and grinned. "I already told you I was
wanted."

"Then maybe I'm coming to my senses after getting a
good night's sleep."

"In that case, you should know that I could have torn out
of here anytime I wanted if it was my intention to get away.
For that matter, I never even had to allow you to come
along with me at all."

"What is your intention here?" Clint asked.

"To finish up my breakfast. You should order some for
yourself. It's the daily special."

Clint maintained his stare until Matt got the hint.

"There's a banker I crossed paths with the last time I

was here," Matt explained. "I was making a withdrawal and he got in the way, so I shot him."

"You killed him?"

"Not so far as I know, but I did hurt him pretty bad. I even heard he could barely form a complete sentence for months after being scared so bad."

"How do you know that?" Clint asked. "Do you keep up with the people you shoot?"

"Not hardly, but I did some checking and I heard that the man was still living here in town. I figured I'd pay him a visit and see about putting his mind to rest."

Clint let out a sigh and motioned for one of the servers to take his order. "I'm sure you could throw some money at him and everything will be just fine."

"I doubt it. That's why I was hoping you'd lend a hand."

"You were hoping that, huh?"

"Sure," Matt replied. "Isn't that why you tagged along?"

TWENTY-ONE

"Is this really necessary?" Matt asked as he stood outside of the livery with his hand resting on his holstered pistol.

Clint stood directly in front of him with his arms hanging loosely at his sides. He wasn't making a move for his own modified Colt, but he could get a grip on the weapon at a moment's notice. For the time being, he simply nodded.

"Yes," Clint replied. "It's necessary."

"Why?"

"As a show of good faith."

"I could get another gun if I wanted, you know," Matt said. "You're not keeping me from anything."

"If you want me to help, you'll do me this favor. Besides, I won't let you out of my sight long enough to visit any firearms stores."

Matt let out a sigh, took his gun from its holster and spun it around so the handle was facing out toward Clint. Handing over the weapon, he said, "Then take it. I don't see why you'd think I'd come all this way to shoot an old man anyhow."

Clint took the gun and stuck it under his own belt. "Thanks for humoring me. Now, would you like to lead the way?"

Matt climbed into his saddle and rode out as Clint was mounting Eclipse. Both men rode through the town of

Lohrens, which was still in the process of waking up and coming to life. Although a few of the locals looked over at them, they didn't seem too interested in where the men were going.

Clint, on the other hand, was plenty interested in seeing where Matt was headed. After rounding a corner, Matt snapped his reins and got moving a bit quicker through a stretch of deserted street. Clint followed behind, but never let his eyes stray too far from Matt.

Plenty of men would have gone to a lot more trouble to distract Clint long enough to take a clean shot at him. Even though Matt hadn't exactly shown himself to be a threat, Clint wasn't in the habit of giving known killers the benefit of the doubt.

He also wasn't in the habit of riding beside known outlaws and letting them lead the way. For some reason, however, Clint was doing just that in the case of Matt Fraley. Despite the fact that common sense would say it was a bad idea, another set of Clint's instincts told him to see it through. Even stronger than those things was the curiosity that made Clint wonder just what the hell was on Matt's mind.

After all the times that Clint had been burned by curiosity, he might have thought that he would have learned his lesson. For that reason, Clint kept Matt where he could see him and waited until Matt rode ahead before taking a few simple measures to disable Matt's gun.

Clint might not have had many of his gunsmithing tools available, but he didn't need much of anything more than years of experience with crafting weapons to make the modifications necessary for him to rest a bit easier. When he looked up again, he saw Matt coming back to where Clint was waiting.

"He's still living there," Matt said.

"You knew where this guy lived?" Clint asked.

Wincing a bit, Matt nodded. "I . . . sort of paid him a visit before robbing the bank. Kind of for insurance."

"What sort of insurance?"

"The kind a man gets when he holds another man's

family hostage and threatens to shoot up his house and home if he don't let me rob that bank."

"Jesus," Clint muttered.

Matt nodded slowly and lowered his head as if he didn't want to look him in the eye. "I know. It was a bad one. That's why it sort of stuck in my mind."

Before Clint could respond to that, the door of the little house Matt had picked out swung open. The hinges creaked loudly and made a grating sound that was soon followed by the knocking of wood against wood. The man who stepped forward wasn't exactly old, but he carried himself as if an additional twenty years had been tacked onto the forty or so that he'd already earned.

The man was skinny, balding, and had a sunken face. A bristly black mustache sprouted from his lip and waggled as he grunted and groaned with the effort of walking outside. Most of that effort was stemming from the fact that he only had one full leg at his disposal and needed to lean on a crutch so he could move.

As soon as the man spotted Matt, his eyes widened and he turned to hustle inside. Considering his predicament, he actually moved pretty fast.

"Pardon us," Matt shouted toward the house. "I wondered if you might be able to—"

Before Matt could finish his question, the one-legged man hobbled back through the door. Along with the crutch, he also brought along a shotgun, which he propped on one arm and then pulled the trigger.

"Holy shit!" Matt shouted as the shotgun roared and sent a plume of smoke into the air.

Clint had pulled Eclipse away from the front of the house as soon as he'd seen that shotgun. Unfortunately, considering the one-legged man's haste, that only put Clint in more danger. Between the man's rush to pull his trigger and his problem balancing on his crutch, the shotgun blast wound up coming closer to Clint than to Matt. Even as the buckshot blazed past Clint's head, the man who'd fired the shotgun was still glaring intently at Matt.

"It's you!" the one-legged man shouted.

Matt's horse had reflexively turned from the house to get away from the shotgun blast. Coming around in a full circle, Matt faced the house again while patting the air with his free hand. "It's not what you think," Matt said.

The one-legged man was trembling, but had collected himself enough to pull the shotgun away from Clint's direction and point it at Matt. His aim might not have been perfect, but it was close enough for the shotgun to put Matt into a world of hurt.

"Just give me a moment to explain," Matt said.

Slowly, the one-legged man shook his head. "No. I remember you. I won't let you hurt me again."

The shotgun in the one-legged man's hands was still shaking, but it wasn't about to be taken away from its target. The look in the man's eyes was full of fear, but there was enough determination mixed in to make his intentions plenty easy to distinguish.

As the roar of the shotgun rolled through the air, the sounds of some distant voices could be heard. Matt's voice cut right through all of that as he leveled his eyes onto the one-legged man and spoke with cool determination.

"Just a minute of your time," Matt said. "That's all I'm asking."

But the other man barely seemed to listen. All he could do was shake his head and tighten his grip on his shotgun.

The next sound to drift through the air was the brush of iron against leather, followed by the metallic click of a pistol's hammer being thumbed back.

"No need to worry about him," Clint said as he pointed the Colt at Matt. "If you let him have a word with you, I promise he won't ever bother you again."

The one-legged man looked over to Clint as if he'd just noticed he was there. "Who are you?" he asked.

"I'm the one who'll pull this trigger if this man so much as thinks about stepping out of line."

Finally, the one-legged man nodded and lowered his shotgun. "Fine. One minute. That's all he gets."

TWENTY-TWO

Despite the fact that he was no longer staring down the barrel of a shotgun, Matt didn't seem any more comfortable once he was inside. In fact, he was more and more uncomfortable as the tension between him and the one-legged man simmered down to a more hospitable level.

Clint watched Matt carefully for any sign that something might be amiss. So far, the only strange thing he could see was the timid way Matt was carrying himself.

The one-legged man set his shotgun down once he was inside his house, and immediately hobbled toward a small shelf nearby. After taking some fresh shells from an old box on that shelf, he reloaded the shotgun and did his best to keep an eye on Matt and Clint as they stepped inside. Considering the fact that he was also balancing on his crutch, it was quite a show.

"You're Matt Fraley," the one-legged man said.

"Yes, sir. I am."

The one-legged man mumbled nervously under his breath while fumbling with the shotgun. Just as he managed to get one of the shells in place, his hand flinched and the shotgun fell from his grasp. He winced in expectation of the loud impact, but slowly opened his eyes when only silence came.

Having been fast enough to lean forward and catch the shotgun before it hit, Clint held the weapon sideways and offered it back to its owner.

"And who're you?" the one-legged man asked.

"My name's Clint Adams."

The one-legged man blinked and let out a breath. "The Gunsmith?"

"That's what some folks call me. I didn't figure on being recognized so easily though."

"Plenty of folks heard of the Gunsmith."

"Yeah," Clint replied. "But most of those spend twenty hours out of the day in a saloon."

That brought a smile to the one-legged man's face. Glancing toward Matt, he asked, "Did that one there tell you who I am?"

"Not by name."

"My name's Abraham Zucker. Of course, he never asked my name when he was holding my family hostage and ruining my life."

"I'm sorry about that," Matt said weakly. "I know it ain't much, but—"

Matt was cut short by a sudden knocking on the front door. Zucker grunted and groaned, but motioned for the other two to step back as he made his way to see who'd done the knocking. Once the door was open and Zucker looked outside, Clint tried to get a look for himself, but couldn't see more than two burly shapes standing on the porch.

"There a problem in there?" one of the burly men asked.

Zucker wasn't quick to answer, but that didn't seem to make any of the other two outside very sympathetic.

TWENTY-THREE

"What the hell were you shooting at, Abe?" one of the men outside asked.

"Shooting?" Zucker replied.

"Yeah. You may be cripple, but we ain't deaf."

Zucker hung his head and said, "I . . . thought I saw something."

The two burly men laughed and leaned forward to get a look inside the house. Even though they had to have seen at least one other stranger inside, they stepped away from the door and threw their last comments over their shoulders as they left.

"Don't fire any more shots in the air," one said.

"If 'n we come back here again, we're takin' that damned shotgun from you," the other added.

Zucker pushed the door shut and dragged himself to a chair next to a small table cluttered with bits of food, a couple books and one chipped ceramic mug. "That outlaw you got there probably coulda shot me dead an' nobody around here would care," he said.

Since there were no more chairs in sight, Clint leaned against a wall. "Why's that?"

"Because of what happened, that's why!" Zucker

snapped. "What the hell good is a bank manager that gives up all his money without a fight?"

"You didn't give up without a fight," Matt said quietly.

Zucker brought his eyes around to glare at Matt as if he was still sighting along the top of his shotgun.

Matt shrugged and added, "Well . . . you didn't." Seeing that Clint was now staring at him as well, Matt told him, "I needed to do some real convincing to get him to work with me."

"Convincing while you had his wife and family held hostage?" Clint asked. "Did that include . . . ?"

Matt shook his head slowly. "I didn't harm a hair on any of their heads. I didn't need to."

"That's right," Zucker replied. "And when everyone came out fine and dandy, all the folks in town started asking where their money went off to. I swear things would've been easier if you would have shot me rather than just hit me in the leg."

Clint looked at Matt and then back to Zucker. Actually, his eyes were drawn more to the stub that had been one of Zucker's legs. "You mean you're the one who took his leg?"

"Not me, but one of the boys riding with my gang," Matt replied. "When we couldn't find the rest of the deposits, we got anxious. I told one of my partners to do some convincing and he let his pistol do his talking."

"Blasted me right in my goddamned kneecap," Zucker growled. "Never had something hurt so bad in my life. Wait a second. I did, actually. After the wound turned sour and the doc had to saw off my leg, that was the worst pain in my life."

Matt winced as he drew in a deep breath.

Digging out a bottle half-full of whiskey, Zucker went on to say, "Even after that, folks around here didn't think it was enough. Those goddamned outlaws hit the bank after the lumber mill deposited their payroll. It took a hell of a while to get that money replaced, and all them mill workers blamed me for not doing my job."

"What did they expect you to do?" Clint asked. "You were robbed. You got shot, for God's sake."

"The manager before me was robbed, too, and he only let the robbers get away with a quarter of the funds in the bank," Zucker explained.

Seeing that Clint was eyeing him sternly, Matt nodded. "We pulled that job, too," he muttered.

"I guess that explains that!" Zucker snapped.

"Did the mill shut down?" Clint asked.

"No."

"Then why the grudge?"

"Because I'm not good with that shotgun and I'm not in charge of anyone's job. At least, I wasn't after I was fired from my own." Holding the whiskey bottle in his hand, Zucker ran his thumb along the smeared glass and said, "Ever since I started drinking this stuff, I barely seem like the educated man I used to be."

Slowly, Matt reached out to take the bottle. Although Zucker put up a bit of a fight, it didn't take much for Matt to pull the bottle away from him. "Trust me," Matt said. "You'll be a lot better off once you're not pouring this poison down your throat."

Once the bottle was out of his grasp, Zucker allowed his empty hand to settle on top of the table like a flower that had been deprived of water. "So what's your business here, anyways? Come by to see about robbing the bank again now that the mill's back on its feet?"

"No," Matt said. "I wanted to—"

"We wanted to thank you," Clint interrupted.

"For what?" Zucker asked.

Judging by the way Matt was staring at Clint, he was about to ask that same question.

"For what you did after the robbery," Clint replied.

After a few seconds of contemplation, Zucker blinked and said, "You mean about that description I gave?"

"There was more than that," Clint pressed.

Although he was quiet for a while, Zucker began to nod. His face brightened as he said, "I described the whole gang of those outlaws right down to the clothes on their backs and the horses they rode. I just didn't think anyone took any notice."

Clint smirked and started walking behind Matt. Pulling Matt up by the back of his shirt, Clint said, "I just needed to stop by here to make sure I was talking to the right man. Since you're the one who had a hand in getting the word out, it's only fair that you get a cut of the reward money for this outlaw's capture."

Zucker brightened up even more, until he seemed to be standing taller on his one leg than the others on their two. "I wasn't thinking about a reward, but it would help out. Would there be enough for me to put a new roof on this place?"

"There'd be enough for you to get a new roof as well as new walls," Matt said. "It seems to me as if you'd be better off packing up and heading to some other town."

At first, Zucker glared at Matt as if he was going to push aside anything the other man said. But soon his face softened, and he lowered his head to nod. "Once my girl moved on, my wife took the boy to Kansas. She had some family there and said it would be easier starting over than putting up with the small-minded folks around here."

"Why didn't you go with them?" Clint asked.

"Because I didn't want these people to think they chased me off. After losing my job and my leg, I didn't want my pride to be taken away next."

Matt laughed under his breath and looked out one of the dirty windows. "From what I've seen of these assholes, they're not worth going through any trouble to impress. And there's no good reason to lose your family. If going through a bit of trouble is what it takes to keep the missus happy, I'd do it. That is, unless she's not worth the effort."

"She's worth it, all right," Zucker said wistfully. "And if you weren't speaking the truth about the rest of it, I would have told you to shut your mouth and mind your own damn business."

"I wouldn't worry about him, Mr. Zucker," Clint said. "He's paying what he owes one way or another."

Zucker looked back and forth between Matt and Clint. With each second that passed, the fire that had been in his eyes dwindled away. "I suppose since he's in your custody and on his way to jail, you'd be right," he said to Clint. "My wife used to send me letters asking to meet up with her again, but I felt too damned foolish to answer. It's been awhile since I got one of those letters."

"Do you honestly think she'll turn you away if you go to see her?" Matt asked.

Reflexively, Zucker glared angrily at Matt. He wasn't able to hold onto that anger for more than another few seconds. "No. I can picture the smile she'd give me already. But . . . packing up and leaving for Kansas . . . that's a lot to bite off."

"What's keeping you here?" Matt asked. "Pride?"

"Missing a leg don't help matters," Zucker grumbled. "Making a trip like that isn't easy for a healthy man. I barely have enough to scrape by, and my wife doesn't have anything to send me. Even if she did have that kind of money, I wouldn't want to ask her for it."

"Your cut of the reward should be more than enough to cover a train ticket and whatever expenses you may have," Clint said. Looking over to Matt, he got a confident nod.

"Unless this bounty hunter's trying to cheat you," Matt added, "there should be enough for you to ditch this house and everything in it to get a fresh start."

Zucker hobbled over to Clint and placed a hand on his shoulder. "This man ain't just some bounty hunter. He's a lifesaver. Hell, even without some windfall of money, I should've gone to Kansas a long time ago."

"After all the trouble you went through to put the word out," Clint replied, "I'll make sure you get your share. Will you be here for a while longer?"

"Yes, sir. I suppose I need to start packing some things for a trip."

"I'll come back as soon as I get that bounty money," Clint said. But Zucker was hardly even listening. Already, the one-legged man was pulling a dusty old carpetbag from under his bed and gathering clothes from various piles to fill it.

When he looked toward Matt, Clint saw the outlaw handing over a rolled-up stack of money. Clint shook his head and quickly motioned for Matt to put the money away. Matt was able to do that a split second before Zucker turned around again.

"If you'd like to earn some more money," Zucker said, "there's plenty more bounties to be collected."

"I think this one will keep me going for a while," Clint replied.

"Maybe, but I'm sure that one there can point you in the direction of the rest of those bandits he rode with. There's been some trouble in these parts lately and I'd wager a few of them are behind it."

"I'll think about it."

"You do that," Zucker said as he made his way to a broken dresser. "You do that."

Since the one-legged man didn't seem to have much more to say, Clint pushed Matt toward the door and they both stepped outside. After closing the door, Clint kept leading Matt past the horses and to a spot across the street where it seemed they could talk without being overheard.

TWENTY-FOUR

"Good thinking back there, but you don't need to keep playing your part when there ain't no audience," Matt said.

"Where'd you get all that money?" Clint asked.

"It's from some of my old jobs just like I told you."

"And I suppose you just sat on that much money and waited to have a change of heart rather than spend it to live like a king on a hacienda somewhere in Old Mexico?"

Matt blinked a few times and then nodded. "Not exactly, but that's what happened."

"Men work their whole lives to scrape together half as much cash as you've been pulling out of your pockets. Outlaws dream about a haul like that from the very first time they pick up a gun. So as soon as you become one of the richest outlaws in history, you decide to start handing it all back?"

"I don't know if I like your tone," Matt said in a low, snarling voice.

"And I don't know if I like the smell of what you've been telling me."

"Nobody forced you to come along, Adams. You don't like what I'm doing? You can get on that high horse of yours and ride away."

Clint shook his head. "I came along for more than just

to lend a hand in your good deeds. By your own admission, you're a man who needs to be watched, and I'm a good one to do the watching."

Walking back to his horse, Matt asked, "Then watch me leave you behind."

Clint reached out with one hand and took hold of Matt's collar. He started to turn the outlaw around, but quickly felt Matt spinning with more than the amount of force in Clint's grasp. Leaning back as fast as he could, Clint was just able to get out of the way of Matt's fist as it lashed around toward his jaw.

Although his first punch had missed, Matt wasn't thrown so easily off balance. He recovered quickly and followed up with another mean hook.

Rather than dodge that punch as well, Clint blocked it with his forearm and then delivered vicious jab to Matt's stomach. The punch landed, but thumped against a mass of thick muscle in Matt's midsection. When Matt reared back to throw a punch intended to separate Clint's head from his shoulders, Clint grabbed Matt's throat with the same speed he might use to draw his Colt from its holster.

"Something's not right with what you've been telling me," Clint said through gritted teeth. "I've known it since we first crossed paths, but could never put my finger on it."

"You're just another goddamn lawman, Adams," Matt replied between forced breaths. "You all just think you're right and the rest of the world is wrong."

"That's wrong and you know it. If I was a lawman, I would've dragged you in just like I told that man back there I was dragging you in."

"So that's what this all boils down to, huh? You really are just another piece-of-shit bounty hunter."

Clint's grip tightened out of pure frustration, but he quickly let Matt go. In the blink of an eye, he slammed the palms of both hands against Matt's chest with enough force to knock him back a few steps. That seemed to rattle Matt just enough to make him pause to catch his breath.

"I saw what you did for that widow and her son," Clint

said. "And I know you weren't doing that just to make an impression on me. I can even see what you intended to do here with this banker, even though you went about it in an odd way."

Matt let out a grunting wheeze and shrugged his shoulders. "What's your point?"

"My point is that something just didn't set well with me, and I know it's the money."

"Plenty of outlaws stash their dollars away, Adams."

"Sure," Clint admitted, "but that's not the case here. There's more to it than that. I could see that much in your eyes the moment I asked you about it just now."

Matt kept his chin up for a few more seconds, but let his gaze fall to the ground after that. "Maybe I didn't stash all that money away."

"So where did it come from?"

"Could be that some of my old gang owed me from when we rode together."

"Could be?" Clint asked.

Eventually, Matt replied, "Or it could be that I took it from them so I could do some good with it."

"And what about those bandits that the banker said were raising hell around here?"

Matt shrugged again. "Could be they're looking to take that money back."

TWENTY-FIVE

When Clint returned to Zucker's house to deliver the money, he wasn't able to enjoy the look on the man's face when he got it.

"Good Lord," Zucker said. "That's a lot more than I thought it would be!"

"Enjoy," Clint replied. "You've earned it."

Zucker's bag was almost packed and his house was already looking as if it was empty. "Thank you so much. I can't tell you how much I appreciate this."

Clint shook the man's hand and did his best to return Zucker's smile, but he wasn't able to be too genuine about it. At least Zucker was too excited about the turn his life had taken to pay much attention to Clint's foul temper. The only thing that made Clint feel a little better was knowing that Matt truly had handed over enough money for Zucker to get to Kansas and start fresh once he got there.

Clint was honestly a bit surprised to find Matt outside waiting for him when he left Zucker's house for the last time.

"What's the matter?" Clint asked as he stormed past the outlaw. "I thought you'd have more good deeds to do."

"There is more for me to do, but I'm not sure I can do it alone."

"You've lied to me already," Clint told him. "From here on, you're on your own."

"You don't mean that."

Clint reeled around to stare directly into Matt's eyes. "Don't I?"

"If you did, you wouldn't have come this far."

"Maybe I made a mistake."

"You're not the only one."

"Spare me the repentant outlaw speech," Clint said as he kept walking to Eclipse so he could climb into the saddle. "I've heard it one too many times already."

"So you just want to part ways? After the way you've stuck to me this far, I'd have thought you wanted to keep a closer watch on me." When he saw Clint snap his reins to get the stallion moving, Matt added, "Either that, or you'd want to turn me over to the law."

Clint pulled back on Eclipse's reins and shifted in his saddle so he could talk while keeping Matt in his line of sight. "You may be a sneaky, double-talking, lying snake, but I don't think you're a killer anymore. Since I'll hunt you down the moment I hear otherwise, I'd say it's in your best interest to keep on the path of the righteous."

After delivering that message, Clint pointed Eclipse's nose toward the street where his hotel was and snapped the reins. The Darley Arabian brought him to the hotel before Clint got a chance to simmer down, and Eclipse seemed more than a little anxious to keep on running. No matter how much he wanted to let the stallion run, Clint climbed down from the saddle and led him to the nearby livery.

The short walk did Clint some good, but he still wasn't back to his normal self by the time he walked into the hotel. Clint traded a quick hello with the brunette at the front desk and stomped up the stairs.

His room was cold and quiet. Rather than light a lantern or think about heating up the room, Clint sat on the edge of the bed and enjoyed a few moments in the calm. Even though he couldn't shake the feeling of being in the eye of a storm, Clint allowed his fists to loosen and his shoulders to come down from around his ears.

After a short time and a few deep breaths, he had to shake his head and smile at how he'd managed to be surprised when Matt Fraley wound up acting the way Clint had expected him to act from the first time they'd met. The very fact that Clint had let Matt out of his sight told him that some part of him still had a bit of faith in the outlaw.

Even so, Matt just had a natural way of getting under Clint's skin.

When someone knocked on the door, Clint kept quiet and hoped for whoever it was to just go away.

Another knock came and Clint ignored it.

When he heard something rattling within the lock and the door swinging slowly open, Clint instinctively reached for the Colt at his side.

Before he drew the pistol, Clint saw a sliver of pale skin framed by curly black hair peeking into the room.

"Oh, sorry," the brunette from the front desk said. "I just wanted to make sure your room was warm enough."

"It's just fine," Clint replied.

"Then . . . do you mind if I stay?"

Clint smiled and stood up. "Actually, that sounds like a great idea."

TWENTY-SIX

The brunette carried a bucket of coal to a small burner in the corner of the room. While fussing with the flame and getting everything situated, she kept glancing at Clint over her shoulder.

"Tell me your name again?" Clint asked.

"Laura."

"Pleased to meet you. My name's Clint."

"I know. I read it off the register."

"I suppose that makes sense," Clint said with an embarrassing laugh.

Now that the coals were in place and heat was beginning to drift up from the burner, Laura stood and walked over to him. She wore a simple brown dress and a cotton shawl over her shoulders. Her thick black hair fell in a curly cascade that made it seem as if it was always in motion.

"You have a pretty smile," Clint told her.

Laura grinned a bit wider and reached out for his shoulders. After moving around behind him, she started to rub his shoulders with a smooth, strong grip. "You look like you've got the weight of the world on your back," she said. "Maybe this will help."

All Clint could do was let out a low grumbling sound as he felt all his worries fade away.

"I'll take that to mean you like it," Laura said.

"You'd be right about that."

After a few more rubs, Clint felt Laura's hands slide over his shoulders so she could reach forward and run her palms against his chest. Clint took hold of her wrists, pulled her arms down a bit more and turned to find himself cheek to cheek with her.

Laura's skin was smooth as silk and her surprised breaths rushed out of her to warm the side of his face. Although Clint could feel her lips brush against his own, he didn't make another move. The longer he waited, the more he could feel Laura's heart pounding against his shoulder blades.

"What are you doing, Mr. Adams?"

"You can call me Clint."

Slowly, Clint stood up and turned around. He kept hold of Laura's wrists, but loosened his grip so he could turn around to face her. Once he was looking directly into her eyes, Clint brought her arms up so her hands could meet behind his neck. In the next instant, Laura locked her fingers together and lifted herself up so she could press her lips urgently against his.

"I have a confession to make," she whispered.

"What's that?"

Laura blinked a few times and shifted nervously so that her breasts and hips wriggled against Clint's body. "I wanted to get this room nice and warm so you wouldn't want to leave it anytime soon. That way, you wouldn't mind spending the night in here."

"That's not much of a confession."

"I wasn't planning on you being alone."

"What a coincidence," Clint said. "I'm not alone right now."

The moment he saw the smile on her face, Clint found the buttons on the side of Laura's dress and undid them one by one. He barely got past the third one before he felt Laura getting restless in his arms. When Clint pulled the rest of the buttons open, Laura let out a surprised gasp.

TWENTY-SEVEN

Her eyes were wide and her hands quickly pulled Clint's shirt open before tugging at his belt. After loosening his belt, she lowered herself to her knees and pulled his jeans all the way down. Laura looked up at Clint as her hands found his growing erection. As the corners of her mouth curled into a smile, she leaned forward and slipped her lips around his cock.

Clint let out a slow breath as he felt her mouth glide all the way down his shaft. Laura's tongue brushed along every inch of him and then began swirling around his penis as she moved her head back and forth. Just then, Clint became very aware of how cold the room was. He guided Laura to her feet and turned her around so her back was to the bed.

She took the direction perfectly and slipped out of her clothes while settling onto the bed. By the time Clint was pulling back the blankets, she was completely naked and eager to slip under the covers. Clint shed the rest of his clothes as well and joined her.

The room's chill had soaked through the blankets, but was soon forgotten once Clint had Laura pressed against him. Her soft skin was warmer than the coals burning nearby, and she warmed him up even more as she kissed

Clint's neck and lips while stroking his cock with one hand.

In moments, Clint was on top of her and Laura's legs were opening wide to accept him. She reached down to guide him into her and let out a soft moan as Clint pushed his hips forward.

Because of the shades drawn down over the windows, only a scant amount of light could get into the room. What little light there was drifted over Laura's breasts, accentuating the large, erect nipples that stood up proudly when she arched her back.

As Clint began thrusting in and out of her, Laura wrapped her arms around him and ran her nails along his back. Every so often, he would thrust deeply inside of her and stay there. Whenever he did that, Clint heard Laura gasp and felt her entire body tense in anticipation of the next time.

Outside the room, several footsteps thumped back and forth in the hallway. A few voices drifted back and forth as well, chatting casually while Clint took hold of Laura's backside in both hands and began pounding into her with increasing force.

Laura bit down on her lower lip to keep from crying out. Just when she thought she had a handle on her passion, Clint would shift his hips or touch her in another way to test her once again.

"Nobody knows you're in here, do they?" Clint asked, picking up on how Laura was reacting to the sound of the others in the hall.

The blush in Laura's cheeks was easy to see, even in the room's dim light. She opened her mouth to say something, but felt Clint's rigid cock drive all the way inside of her in a way that pushed all the air from her lungs. She let out a little groan and then immediately covered her mouth with her hand.

"No," she whispered. "I'm supposed to be preparing for—" She was cut off again as Clint ran his hand along her thigh while thrusting powerfully between her legs.

"What were you saying?" Clint asked.

"Nothing. Just don't stop."

Clint pumped into her once more before straightening his back so he was kneeling on the bed. The covers fell away from them, revealing Laura's naked body beneath him. Her stomach heaved with excited breaths and her hair spilled loosely over her. When he saw her move her hands, Clint thought she was going to try and cover herself. Laura surprised him by slipping one hand between her legs to rub herself in a spot just above where he'd entered her.

As Clint kept pumping into her, Laura rubbed herself until her eyes were clenched shut and her breaths were coming in short, excited bursts. Soon, Clint could feel her tightening around him as she was overtaken by a powerful orgasm.

While Laura was still trembling beneath him, Clint leaned forward so he could hold her breasts with both hands. Her soft, rounded curves filled his hands and her nipples pressed against his palms. Squirming and moaning softly, Laura opened her legs wide and wriggled her hips in time to Clint's thrusts.

Soon, Clint felt his own climax approaching, and he kept pounding into her until it arrived. Laura enjoyed the feel of his weight upon her so much that she whimpered with the pleasure of another smaller climax of her own.

Feeling his strength drain out of him, Clint was just able to roll onto the bed next to Laura while letting out a satisfied breath. In the space of another few seconds, however, Laura was no longer beside him. Clint looked over just in time to see her bare, rounded backside as she hopped out of bed and bent to retrieve her clothes.

"You don't have to go just yet," Clint said.

"Actually, I do. I'm not supposed to be in here."

"If anyone asks, I'll swear you left the room perfectly clean."

Laura pulled on her dress, but only bothered to fasten a few of the buttons. When she leaned down to touch his face, her breasts swayed perfectly beneath the loosely fit-ted fabric. "You're sweet," she said while patting his cheek. "But all the explaining in the world won't do the trick if my job isn't done before the owner gets back."

Clint leaned back and folded his hands behind his head. He never grew tired of watching a woman get dressed, and he wasn't about to start now. Laura left after blowing him a kiss.

Just as he was about to drift off for a little nap, Clint was awakened by the sudden opening and closing of his door. Laura jumped back into his room and had a look on her face that was the polar opposite of the one that had been there when she'd left.

"You need to come out here," she said in a rush. "Your friend is about to get shot."

TWENTY-EIGHT

Clint threw on his clothes, pulled on his boots, strapped his holster around his waist and was out the door in the blink of an eye.

Laura was in the hall and pointing toward the front door of the hotel, but Clint didn't need much direction to know where the source of the trouble was. All he needed to do was look for the small crowd that had gathered outside the hotel's front window.

"What's going on?" Clint asked as he hurried down the stairs.

Laura stood at the window and shifted back and forth to try and get a look past some of the people standing on the other side of the glass. "Some men rode down the street and started yelling. Someone else came out and then everyone drew their guns."

"When the hell did all this happen?"

"While we were . . ." She paused and looked around before adding, "One of the maids told me about it when I was leaving your room."

Pushing open the door, Clint managed to clear a path for himself so he could step outside. From there, he stepped between some of the gawkers on the boardwalk so he could get a look at what was going on.

The street was empty apart from three men on horse-back and one on foot. The man without the horse was Matt and he was currently staring down the barrels of all three of the others' guns. Matt spoke to the closest of the other three, but neither of them was talking loudly enough for Clint to hear them.

Clint stepped forward, but stopped at the edge of the boardwalk. The moment Matt looked in his direction, Clint found himself under the other three's scrutiny as well.

"Is that the asshole you're riding with?" the lead man on horseback asked loudly.

Matt looked over to Clint and nodded.

Raising his voice even more, the man on horseback added, "I suppose he helped you rob us blind!"

Just then, four more men rounded the corner closest to the hotel and fanned out into a straight line. Clint recognized one of those men as Marshal Lind.

"You men lower your guns!" Lind shouted. "If anyone's been robbed, you take it up with me. But if anyone fires a shot, my men and I will make you wish you never stepped foot in this town."

The only rider who'd raised his voice kept his gun arm extended as he shifted his eyes back and forth between Matt, Clint and the newly arrived lawmen. The other two riders kept their guns drawn and never took their eyes off of the lead rider.

"Don't push this, gentlemen," Lind announced. "Settle your differences in a civilized way or you can talk it out while you're in jail. You won't like the third option."

The lead rider smirked when he heard that and nodded to the other two men behind him. Once he started lowering his pistol, the other two riders followed suit.

"No need for all this fuss," the leader said. "I guess this fucking town caters to thieves and killers, that's all."

The lawmen didn't budge. Although Lind's eyes were firmly set, the deputies flanking him looked more uneasy with every second that passed.

Holstering their guns, the three riders took hold of their reins.

"Good," Lind said. "Now you can—"

"I'll find you, asshole," the lead rider said to Matt. "There ain't nowhere for you to run." With that, he snapped his reins, put the lawmen behind him and got his horse running down the street.

A few of the deputies leaned forward as if they were preparing to feel the kick of their weapons, but Lind restrained them by holding both arms out to his sides. "Let 'em go. So long as they leave without a mess, I don't care what they say."

Clint stepped into the street and saw one of the deputies take aim at him. The marshal spotted Clint right away, shoved the deputy's gun down and then motioned for his men to follow him back around the corner. Since the lawmen didn't seem interested in pursuing the matter further, Clint didn't press it.

"Who were those men?" Clint asked as he walked up to Matt.

Judging by the look on Matt's face, he could have been out for a stroll after a hearty lunch. "Remember those fellows I mentioned in regards to the money?"

"Yes."

"There you go."

"How did they find you?"

Matt grinned and replied, "Losing as much as they did tends to be one hell of a good inspiration to look. Have you eaten yet?"

"Are you out of your mind?"

Matt crossed the street, stepped onto the boardwalk and headed toward a restaurant on the corner. Around him, the crowd was already starting to drift back to what they'd been doing before the commotion. "Everything turned out fine," Matt replied. "Crying about it won't do any good."

"And you think those men are just going to ride off so they can forget why they showed up in the first place?"

Matt waited until Clint was directly in front of him before saying, "Most any day out of the week, I'd steal a horse if I had to just so I could tear after those cocksuckers and Ben knows that."

"So what were you proposing to do after being held at gunpoint in the middle of the street by those men?"

Motioning toward the restaurant, Matt said, "I'm hungry. How about you?"

TWENTY-NINE

Clint and Matt got a cold roast beef sandwich thrown at each of them within moments after entering the restaurant. The place was fairly busy, and no more than a couple of the people inside tossed a sideways glance at either of them. It seemed as if the servers would have treated Clint and Matt the same way whether or not they'd been fresh from a standoff.

By the time he'd taken his first bite of the sandwich, Clint asked, "You said that man's name was Ben?"

Matt nodded and stuffed his mouth full.

"As in Ben Jarrett?"

"You've heard of him?" Matt asked.

"In passing. Actually, I'd just seen his face in the marshal's office while I was flipping through some bounty notices."

"Were his in date at least?"

"Oh yes. He's also worth more than you."

"Not according to that banker," Matt replied with a smirk.

Ignoring the jolly tone in Matt's voice, Clint said, "Ben Jarrett has buried plenty of men down in New Mexico."

"And that marshal still didn't recognize him. That's a damn shame."

Clint kept his eyes on Matt until the outlaw decided to shift his attention back to his plate. "Was he talking to you about that money?"

Matt nodded. "It came up once or twice."

"What did you tell him?"

"To go steal some more if it meant so much to him. Before you ask, he didn't take too kindly to my suggestion."

"What do you intend to do about this?" Clint asked.

"I could go to the law, but that wouldn't be such a good idea. Even if the marshal knew his ass from a hole in the ground, he wouldn't stand a chance against Ben. What I intend to do is to wait for him to get impatient and let his guard down so I can see that he gets what's coming just like the other folks I've visited."

"You delivered those other folks enough money to start a new life," Clint pointed out. "As well intentioned as that may have been, it's still blood money."

"All money's got blood on it, Adams. Don't sit there and pretend you didn't know that."

Clint knew that all too well. In the end, money was only as good or bad as the people who had ahold of it at the time. Still, there was something that Clint couldn't justify no matter how hard he tried to think it through.

"You handed out that money knowing a killer was looking for it?" Clint asked. "Doesn't something about that strike you as wrong?"

"I think they'll put it to better use than Ben Jarrett would. Besides, thieves set their sights on folks no matter what they got, who they are or where they live. Those folks can either be afraid or they can live their lives. Besides, Ben's after me. He doesn't care about going back to rob the folks we already robbed."

"If Ben knew those folks were rich, he might regain some interest in them."

Matt winked and washed down some more of his sandwich with the water he'd been given. Once his mouth was empty, he said, "Ben won't be able to harm nobody when he's dead."

THIRTY

Matt Fraley had been right about at least one thing: Ben Jarrett was most definitely losing his patience.

After riding out of town and circling back again, he and one of his men left their horses tied to a post two streets from the spot where they'd had words with Matt and then walked straight back to that same hotel. Ben walked with a confident stride and an easy smile on his face. He might have been considered a handsome man if not for the deadly gleam in his eyes that marked him the same way a rattlesnake was marked by the colors on its back.

A few paces from the hotel's front door, Ben glanced to the man beside him and said, "Keep your mouth shut and follow my lead."

"What if Matt's in there?"

"I told you to keep your mouth shut, Danny. Are you going deaf?"

The other man was an inch or so taller than Ben and was missing the bottom halves of three front teeth. Despite the battle scars he wore in his mouth and on his face, he deferred to Ben without so much as a word in his own defense.

"If he's in there, we'll deal with him," Ben said. "You

saw them laws that were out here before. We can walk through them without getting our boots dirty."

Danny nodded and pulled open the hotel door so Ben could step inside.

Laura was watching the door intently and couldn't hide the fear in her eyes when she saw the two men step inside. "Aren't you . . . ?"

"We're here to inquire about one of the men who was causing the stir outside your door," Ben said. "Is he a guest here?"

"Umm . . . I shouldn't . . ."

"You sure as hell should," Danny snarled as he lunged forward to grab hold of Laura's arm. "If you don't loosen that tongue of yers, I'll cut it from your damn head."

Ben eased up to the desk and took in the sight of the pretty brunette being pulled across the top of it. Letting out a sigh, he tapped Danny's arm. That was enough to make Danny loosen his grip. "You'll have to excuse my friend," Ben said. "He's a little worked up after that display I'm sure you saw in the street earlier."

"Marshal Lind is sure to come by and check up on us soon," Laura said.

"Is he really, sweetheart?" Ben asked.

Although she tried to keep a straight face, Laura was barely even able to keep her eyes on either of the two men. She didn't speak. She didn't nod. She didn't shake her head. All Laura could do was lower her head.

The more he saw her squirm, the more Ben seemed to like it. "That was just a question, honey, but you did a fine job of answering it. You've got too honest of a face to pull off a bluff."

Someone walked through the front door and headed for the stairs. "Are there any more newspapers?" he asked.

Since Laura was still at a loss for words, Ben broke the silence with "I just took the last one. Sorry."

The man on the stairs had a full head of silver hair and didn't seem too interested in prolonging the conversation since he was already climbing the stairs. "Have one sent up to my room when you can," he replied.

"Will do." Turning to Laura, Ben added, "I'd say that's about all the help you're gonna get."

"What do you want?" Laura asked.

"An answer to my question. Is that other fella that was outside a while ago a guest here? His name's Matt Fraley."

Laura kept her eyes lowered, but jumped as soon as she felt Danny take rough hold of her chin.

"Yes," she blurted. "His name's right there on the register."

Without glancing down at the large book that lay open on the desk in front of him, Ben said, "I'll take your word for it. Is he with anyone else?"

Laura shook her head. "He's in a room all by himself. I swear."

Ben nodded and took that opportunity to look at the register. He flipped one page back, spotted Matt's name and then tapped his finger to another name written above it. "Clint Adams? Did I read that right?"

Danny glanced quickly down at the register, but regarded it the way a dog might regard the inner workings of a clock. "Is that what it says?"

"Sure enough," Ben told him. "I thought I recognized that face. You see, Danny, Mr. Adams was on the street earlier as well. I've seen him a few times before at poker games in West Texas." Looking to Laura, Ben asked, "Adams came here with Matt?"

She didn't say a word.

"Remember, sweetie, there's no lying to me."

"They checked in at around the same time," she said. "You can see that much for yourself."

"Yeah, I suppose I can see that much for myself." Ben brushed the back of his hand along Laura's face and then slid the hand all the way down to graze along the side of her breast.

Laura recoiled and reflexively swatted Ben's hand away.

Ben smiled and stepped back. "Can you do me a favor, honey? I'd like you to deliver a message to my friend Matt and his friend Adams."

"I don't know if I'll be speaking to them again."

Picking up on the tremor in her voice, Matt shook his head and tossed a grin to Danny. "Don't worry about that. You won't have to say a word to deliver this message."

With that, Ben drew his pistol, extended his arm and pulled his trigger. His bullet exploded from the gun's barrel and tore a gaping hole between Laura's startled eyes.

THIRTY-ONE

Clint was walking out of the restaurant when he heard the shot. The instant he figured it was coming from the direction of the hotel, he broke into a run with Matt not too far behind him. Before he got close enough to get a good look at the hotel, he spotted two of the men that had been in the street with Matt.

Ben was climbing into his saddle when he spotted Clint. Tossing a quick wave over his shoulder, he settled in his saddle, snapped the reins and got moving.

"Son of a bitch," Clint muttered. He was in mid-stride when he saw the gun in Ben's hand.

It was pure reflex that caused both Clint and Matt to draw their own pistols. They only had to wait a second before Ben took a shot at them and rode down the street. Clint returned fire, but knew the men were already out of pistol range.

Matt fired as well, but the snarl on his face made it plain to see that he was doing so more out of anger than the desire to hit anything. "That son of a bitch is just trying to get under my skin," he said once the roar of his gun had faded a bit.

"Well, he's done a hell of a job," Clint said. "I'm getting my horse and chasing him down. Are you coming with me?"

"You couldn't keep me away."

Both men ran for the livery, but soon found themselves snarled up in a thick group of people gathered around the front of the hotel and spilling out of it. There were too many of them screaming and carrying on for them all to be reacting to the couple of shots that had gone off.

"What is it?" Clint asked as he nearly knocked one local down.

The younger man staggered, but kept trying to run away. "There's a dead woman in there," he said while pointing toward the hotel.

Clint felt the bottom of his stomach drop as he shoved through the crowd to get to the front door of the hotel. Before he got the door open, he could smell the stink of burnt gunpowder and spilled blood in the air. When the door had only cracked an inch or so open, he could see the blood staining the wall behind the front desk.

"God damn it," Clint snarled when he saw Laura on the floor.

He didn't need to see any more to know she was gone.

Clint didn't even realize he was moving again until he was outside.

Matt was in his saddle and holding Eclipse's reins in his hands while waiting for Clint in the street. The Darley Arabian was fussing under Matt's control, but calmed down the moment he caught sight of Clint heading his way.

In a matter of seconds, Clint was in his own saddle and snapping his reins to get Eclipse running down the street.

Matt caught up to him and kept pace so he could look over and ask, "Was someone shot in there?"

"Yes."

"A woman?"

Clint had to pause before saying, "Yes. It was the brunette who worked at the front desk."

"Jesus Christ."

"Would Ben go to that much trouble to get under your skin?" Clint asked.

"That's his way of telling me it was a mistake to steal from him and then run away."

Clint pulled hard on his reins and steered Eclipse around a corner. Once he saw the edge of town drawing closer, he leaned down and tapped his heels against the Darley Arabian's sides. "Now it's Ben that's made the mistake."

Matt nodded solemnly and did his best to keep up with Eclipse. Every so often, he would point in the direction he thought Ben had gone. There wasn't much guesswork involved, however, since the town of Lohrens wasn't big enough to have many places for escaping killers to hide. Although Clint was a little ways behind Ben and Danny, the dust the others had kicked up was still swirling in the air. Without any buildings nearby that were large enough to hold two men and two horses, Clint followed the dust trail to the open range outside of town.

"Halt!" someone shouted from behind Clint and Matt.

Clint twisted around in his saddle to see who'd shouted loudly enough to be heard over the thunder of Eclipse's hooves. He was surprised to find Marshal Lind running down the middle of the street behind him.

"Too little too late," Clint said as he turned back around to steer Eclipse out of Lohrens.

Matt grinned and snapped his reins to keep up. "Looks like we might have a real chase on our hands," he shouted. "It's been awhile, but I'm up for it!"

THIRTY-TWO

Matt wasn't the only one who was a bit rusty at outrunning the law. Once he heard the enthusiasm in Matt's voice, Clint took a second to think if he'd ever done what he was in the process of doing right now. He couldn't think of an instance offhand, but Clint was also a little too busy to give the matter more than a moment of consideration.

While one part of his head sifted through those thoughts, the rest of him was rattling and churning like a steam engine's piston that was about to explode from its casing. Clint did his best to keep from dwelling on the fresh memory of Laura laying on that floor. Thinking of that would make him too angry to keep his wits about him. There would be plenty of time for Clint to be angry once he got his hands on Ben Jarrett.

As Lohrens faded behind him, Clint had no trouble at all in spotting Ben and Danny. Their other riders were well ahead of him, but their horses standing in the open couldn't be missed. Clint knew better than to bite on that bait right away and pulled Eclipse sharply to the right.

Before Matt could say anything about the sudden turn, Clint looked over to him and said, "You take the left."

Matt nodded and veered off in that direction. Once they'd split off, the other two of Ben's riders came out from where they were waiting so they could charge forward before they were flanked.

Even though Clint hadn't been heading directly for those other two, he'd gotten close enough to make them nervous. Clint grinned and got Eclipse moving even faster. Nothing was more satisfying than spoiling one man's bluff with an even bigger one of his own. Now that all four of the outlaw riders had shown themselves, Clint let out a sharp whistle aimed at Matt.

The outlaw turned quickly to see what Clint wanted. The moment he saw Clint waving to him, Matt pulled his reins so he could meet up with Clint and ride once more at Eclipse's side.

By this time, Ben and his other riders had formed a single group. Those four now charged toward Clint and Matt as a few distant gunshots cracked through the air. Knowing he was well out of pistol range for the moment, Clint wasn't too concerned with the wild shots. There was, however, one other group to worry about.

The first few times Clint had checked over his shoulder, he hadn't seen one trace of Marshal Lind or any of his deputies. Now that he and Matt had been able to saddle up and race out of town, another group of riders was also charging out of Lohrens. This third group may have been only two strong, but Clint could see a few others breaking away from the town's limits so they could meet up with the original pair.

"That's either the law," Matt shouted, "or more of Ben's boys."

"It's the law," Clint said.

"You sure about that?"

"Yeah. They're not shooting at us."

Matt laughed once and added, "Not yet, anyway. It's probably a good idea to not let them catch up."

As much as he hated to admit it, Clint agreed. And since he knew he hadn't done anything that warranted being chased by the law, he didn't have any trouble in giving

Eclipse the order to bolt ahead like a bullet from the barrel of a gun.

As the Darley Arabian tore over the ground between Clint and Ben, Matt started to fall behind. No matter how much he whipped his own horse, Matt wasn't able to maintain the other stallion's pace. Rather than kill his horse in the futile hopes of winning the race, Matt took the rifle hanging from his saddle and laid it across his lap.

Clint reached down with one hand to carefully take the modified Colt from its holster. Every muscle in his body moved in time to Eclipse's steps, but he still wasn't about to risk dropping his gun before firing it. Since he knew the Darley Arabian stallion and the Colt as well as he knew his own arms and legs, Clint never had to take his eyes off of the oncoming riders to get the pistol in hand and take aim.

As the two groups closed in on each other, the wild firing from Ben's side tapered off. Clint took a quick look over his shoulder to find Matt a little ways behind him with a rifle against his shoulder. Turning even farther around, Clint could see that the group he figured to be lawmen were so far behind that they might have already given up on trying to catch him.

Clint hadn't yet turned back around when he heard a shot crack through the air. Reflexively, he ducked down and snapped his head around to get a look at Ben and the other three riders. A bullet hissed through the air close enough for Clint to hear it, but not so close that he was afraid of getting hit.

Bringing up the Colt, Clint sighted down the barrel and fired a shot at the outlaw riders. He kept his aim low enough to make his intentions clear, but not low enough to knock anyone from his saddle.

Sure enough, that one round was enough to split two of the four riders away from the rest. It also made the outlaws jumpy enough to start answering back before Clint and Matt got any closer.

Shots crackled from Ben and his men, sounding like

corks popping directly in front of Clint's nose. A few rounds whipped by Clint, but most of them either fell short or were too wild to make their presence felt. Matt fired his rifle a few times, causing one of Ben's men to wobble in his saddle and fire his next shot straight out to his right.

Even though all the horses were running at a full gallop, Clint was focused so intently on Ben and the other three riders that it didn't seem as if they were getting any closer. Suddenly, it all rushed in on him as he could now make out the sneers on the men's faces.

Clint sighted along the top of his Colt to take a few shots in earnest. He'd lost count of how many shots the men had fired, but he knew they'd burned through a good amount of their ammunition before he and Matt even got within range.

The next shot Clint fired was at the rider to Ben's left. That one was taking aim at him and must have been close to pulling his trigger. Clint fired first and felt the Colt buck against his palm. As soon as he saw the rider flinch, Clint shifted his aim to one of the others.

Matt was firing as well, and he managed to drop one of the riders from his saddle with a pair of shots from his rifle.

As the two groups of horses drew closer together, the firing was coming more and more from Matt and Clint. Ben had saved a few rounds for this spot, but his men were already in dire need of a reload. One of them was forced to holster his pistol and try to take another from his belt while also struggling to keep hold of his reins.

"All right!" Ben shouted. "Break off!"

With that command, all three of the remaining outlaw riders made a sharp turn away from Clint and Matt. No two of them chose the same direction, which created a thick cloud of dust as all three of their horses kicked up clumps of dirt while scrambling to turn.

Although Clint could see what the riders were doing, he was moving too quickly to do anything other than try to steer Eclipse to a spot where he wouldn't smack against another horse or ride straight into a stray round of gunfire.

Where everything had been playing itself out slowly in Clint's mind before, the scene was suddenly launched into a confusing mess of swirling dust, thundering hooves, shouting voices and flying lead.

Shots were still being fired at them, but Clint and Matt could no longer tell where they were coming from.

Just as Clint was beginning to sort through the mess, he saw a man climbing to his feet no more than three steps in front of Eclipse's nose. It was all Clint could do to pull the reins and turn Eclipse away before trampling the other man. Although he did manage to steer around him, Clint was forced to bring the Darley Arabian to a stop.

THIRTY-THREE

For a moment, Clint couldn't tell if Matt was nearby or was still on Ben's trail. He put that aside for the moment when he realized that the man he'd almost trampled was one of the riders who'd been shot from his saddle.

The man's left arm was hanging limply from his shoulder, and his clothes were stained by both blood and dirt. "Go to hell!" he shouted as he tried to grab for a gun sticking from his belt. That motion was more than enough to bring a pained wince to his face as he grabbed a bloody wound in his side.

"Your friends left you behind," Clint said. "How about you tell me where they're headed so I can show them the error of their ways?"

The other man flashed a dirty grin as he said, "They left but we ain't alone."

Following the man's eyes, Clint looked back toward Lohrens and saw the other group of riders that he'd pegged as lawmen. They weren't quite close enough to make out the whites of their eyes, but they were making steady progress.

"Far as those lawmen know," the wounded man said, "you and Matt are the ones that shot that bitch in the hotel."

Clint's eyes narrowed as the image of Laura's dead

body was brought back into his mind. "Come on," he said while extending a hand down to the man. "Unless you want to take your chances with the law."

"Maybe I will."

"And maybe they'll hang you once someone from that hotel speaks up about you being there before Matt or I even showed our faces anywhere near that dead woman."

The smug look on the man's face slowly started to fade as Clint's words sank in. Eventually, he started glancing over his shoulder toward the lawmen as if he was no longer glad to see them coming. "You're just gonna shoot me when you get the chance."

"I've got my chance right now," Clint said while holding his gun hand out for the man to take rather than drawing his Colt.

"Careful," the man grunted. "I got a—"

But the man's warning was cut short as Clint took hold of his arm and hauled him up onto Eclipse's back without so much as a hint of regard for the fresh wounds. The man let out a pained yelp as all of his weight strained against his wounded shoulder while stretching out the bullet wound in his side. By the time Clint lifted him into the saddle, the man dangled unconsciously from his hand.

Clint grunted with the effort of holding the man up. Thankfully, he only needed to do it for another second or two before draping the man across Eclipse's back. Judging by the way the wounded man nearly flopped off the stallion, Clint was certain the guy had passed out from the pain.

Holding the unconscious man in place with one arm, Clint kept hold of his reins in his free hand and snapped them to get Eclipse moving again. Before he could think too long about how he could keep from being shot at by the panicky lawmen, Clint saw another horse ride up to him.

"Anyone send for the cavalry?" Matt asked.

"Where's Ben and the others?"

"I could only follow one for a little bit before losing him

in some trees. The others were long gone by the time I doubled back."

"And you don't think you could have caught up in time?" Clint asked.

Matt shook his head. "They would have each run for miles before meeting up somewhere else they'd picked out beforehand. It's a good move to make an escape and it's damn effective. I should know, since I'm the one who taught it to Ben."

"Then you know where Ben's going."

Matt shook his head. "The whole beauty of that move is that nobody knows where it's headed other than the men doing the running. It's different every time. That way, it can be used plenty of times."

"All right, save me the sales pitch," Clint said.

"But it looks like you've already got the answer to our little problem," Matt said while nodding toward the unconscious man laying across Eclipse's back. "I may not know the details of where Ben's headed, but you can sure bet that fella does."

Clint pulled in a breath and turned to look at the lawmen who were closing in on them. Their horses were only building up more speed now that the riders could tell that Clint and Matt had come to a stop.

"They won't be sitting still for long, Adams," Matt said. "If you want to be sure to give Ben enough time to make a clean getaway, then just head on over to those lawmen and try to explain what happened."

All Clint had to do was think once more about Laura's wide, dead eyes and the decision was made. With a snap of the reins, he turned his back once more to Lohrens and rode away from the approaching lawmen. It took a bit of time for Eclipse to build up speed, but the Darley Arabian was soon able to give Marshal Lind a chase.

As he rode, Clint shook the wounded man by the collar. Between that and the motion of Eclipse's strides, the man was quickly rattled awake.

"What the . . . ," the wounded man groaned. As soon as he saw where he was and what was happening, he grabbed onto the first thing he could reach. Holding onto the lower edge of the saddle wasn't nearly enough to put his mind to rest.

"Tell me where to find Ben or I'll drop you on your fool head," Clint said once he saw the wounded man start to squirm.

"I don't know, for Christ's sake!"

"Fine. I don't need the extra weight anyway." When Clint slapped his hand on the man's back, he thought he heard whimpering coming from the wounded outlaw.

"Head south!" the wounded man shouted. "There's a camp by a lake! I'll take you right to it!"

"That's more like it," Clint replied.

THIRTY-FOUR

Even with the extra weight on his back, Eclipse was able to put the lawmen behind him and keep them there until Clint was able to find a way to shake them. After a few sharp turns through some trees and a quick circle around a lake, Clint was no longer able to see or hear a trace of the posse. Before too long, Matt joined up with him once again.

"They're headed back to town," Matt said as he brought his horse to a stop. "A pretty sorry excuse for a posse if you ask me."

"Nobody asked you," Clint replied.

While Matt knew well enough to keep quiet, the wounded man wasn't so smart.

"Ain't much more than a lawdog yourself, huh?" the wounded man grunted. "That figures."

Without a word to announce his intentions, Clint pushed the wounded man over Eclipse's back until he began sliding to the hard earth below. At the last second, Clint tightened his grip on the man's belt to keep him from falling all the way.

"What was that you were saying?" Clint asked.

All the wounded man could get out was a couple of gurgling moans.

Matt shook his head as he climbed down from his saddle and walked over to Eclipse. "All right, big man," he said as he reached out to get ahold of the outlaw dangling from Eclipse's back. "Let's get you down from there before you talk yourself into a cracked skull."

Clint leaned down so he could work with Matt to get the wounded man off of Eclipse and onto the ground. Once that was done, Clint swung down himself and fished the spyglass from his saddlebag. He held the spyglass to one eye and pointed it toward the direction from which they'd come.

"See anyone?" Matt asked.

Swinging the spyglass back and forth, Clint finally replied, "Nope."

"I suppose we're out of that marshal's jurisdiction. Either that, or he's too damn lazy to ride for more than a few minutes to catch a killer."

"Or maybe he knows we're not the killers," Clint added. "There's always the possibility that he caught Ben's trail and is after him right now."

The wounded outlaw let out a grunting laugh. "Yeah. And maybe their horses sprouted wings and flew off."

"Shut up," Matt said.

Clint didn't show it, but he figured the wounded man was more or less on the right track. He put away the spyglass and took the rope that hung from his saddle. "Time for you to earn your keep," Clint said. "Where do we head now?"

"First I need to see a doctor," the wounded man snapped. "If'n I don't stop bleeding, I can't say shit."

"We're not making camp," Clint said. "The only reason we stopped was to get our bearings and sit you up properly. Oh, and one more thing." With that, Clint slapped his free hand against the wounded man's side and belt, to find and toss away two more pistols. After that, he gathered up the man's hands and started looping rope around them.

The wounded man gritted his teeth and locked eyes with Matt. "You thieving son of a bitch."

Matt chuckled under his breath before replying, "So that's what it means for the pot to call the kettle black."

"We may steal from everyone else, but we don't steal from each other. That's just plain cowardly."

"You know what's cowardly?" Clint asked as he cinched in the knot to keep the man's wrists bound together. "Shooting an unarmed woman in cold blood. A man doesn't get much more yellow than that."

The wounded man grumbled and looked away. His shoulder was still misaligned, but his eyes were glazed over. After all that pain, Clint figured the man probably wasn't feeling much of anything at the moment. Just to wake him up, Clint gave the man's wounded shoulder a gentle pat. When the wounded man's eyes snapped open and he pulled in a quick breath, Clint motioned for Matt to come over and help him.

"Let's get our friend into the saddle so he can ride like a man instead of a bedroll," Clint said.

Between the two of them, Clint and Matt were able to get the man onto Eclipse's back. Clint climbed up next so that the wounded man was behind him.

"You want to tell me your name?" Clint asked.

The man held his tongue.

"His name's Dell," Matt said. "At least, that's what everyone calls him."

"All right, Dell. Where's this camp you were talking about?"

Clint wasn't sure if it was the pain from his wounds, the loss of blood, or just a general feeling of hopelessness, but Dell lost his attitude and slumped like a scarecrow on a post.

"Due south," Dell said. "But they may not even be there anymore. We were just supposed to meet up and ride out again."

"I guess we'll have to take our chances. You ready, Matt?"

Already in his saddle, Matt nodded. "As I'll ever be. You still want me to tag along?"

"Why wouldn't I? You've come this far. Are you done handing out that money?"

"What?" Dell grunted. "You gave away that money? It don't belong to you!"

"It doesn't belong to you," Matt said. "And it doesn't belong to Ben, either."

Dell shook his head and muttered, "Fucking bastard."

Wearing a wide smile on his face, Matt rode up next to Eclipse. When he patted Dell on the back, it wasn't with any more force than he would use to greet a friend. That small impact on Dell's wounds, however, was enough to drain all the color from his face.

"You just keep flapping those lips, Dell," Matt said. "It'll make me feel better about shooting you in the first place."

Clint laughed at the pitiful squeaks coming from the outlaw behind him. "All right, Dell," he said before Matt got any more ideas. "Lead on so we can get you to that doctor you wanted."

THIRTY-FIVE

The spot Clint wound up at was pretty much as Dell had described it. There were some winding trails and a lake. There was even a flat stretch of ground that would have made a real good place to bed down for the night. After taking a look around, Clint looked over his shoulder at Dell's pale face.

"Is this the spot?" Clint asked.

Dell looked around and nodded. "I told you they wouldn't be here. You'd better still hold up your end of this deal."

Matt had already climbed from his saddle so he could get a closer look at the ground. "These tracks are still pretty fresh," he said while staring at a cluster of imprints in the dirt. "No way of knowing where they lead, though."

"Answer my question, dammit," Dell croaked. "Are you holding up your end of the deal or not? I need a goddamn doctor."

Clint looked around and then nodded. "You'll get your doctor."

"Fine, then. There's a town not too far down the way. It ain't too big, but there should be a—"

"There's a town even closer," Clint cut in. "It's called Lohrens. Perhaps you've heard of it."

Dell was quiet, but he was squirming enough to almost slip off of Eclipse's back. "You take me there and they'll arrest me."

"That's the idea."

"God damn you. God damn both of you."

"If that upsets you so much, maybe we should just leave you here," Matt offered. "I'm sure you can inch your way along to a safer town in a day or two. Or maybe a week or two considering your injury."

Clint turned Eclipse around and flicked the reins. He knew Ben and the others weren't about to show up if they weren't already there. Already, Clint was feeling foolish for taking the gamble that Ben would wait around to see if Dell might be able to meet up with him.

"I'll take him back into town," Clint said.

But Matt remained at Clint's side. "Alone?"

"I don't see a need for both of us to go."

"You could use a scout," Matt said. "After what you've done to help me so far, the least I can do is make sure you don't wind up in a jail cell for what Ben Jarrett did to that woman."

"You don't want to keep after Ben yourself?" Clint asked.

"Sure I do. But, truth be told, I think I stand a better chance of finding him with you than without you."

Clint nodded. "All right, then. If you'd really like to help, I can think of something that would be a whole lot more useful than scouting."

Marshal Lind was still kicking himself for losing sight of all those horses. He'd had a hard enough time pulling together enough deputies to form a posse, but keeping them riding toward a gun battle was even tougher. When the outlaws had scattered like buckshot from a shotgun barrel, some of his deputies had even seemed glad.

Now, as he circled the town and led his men along a few broken trails, Marshal Lind felt as if he'd wasted his time in trying to hunt down the killers. The woman in the hotel was still dead and the murderers were out of the town's limits. Lind's job was done. It was time to go home.

"Marshal!" shouted one of the few deputies who were still enthusiastic about being out there. "I see someone!"

"Where?" Lind asked.

"Right there. You think it's one of those men we're after?"

Lind squinted into the distance as more of his men gathered around. "He's coming this way."

While Lind watched, the rider they'd spotted stopped at a spot less than a hundred and fifty yards away. The marshal didn't like the way the man was perched in his saddle, but before he could say or do anything about it, the rider had already fired a shot at him.

"That's enough of that," Lind said. "Gather up anyone you can find and follow me. We'll either bring that gunman in or send him across the state line with his tail between his legs."

The deputies who were eager to continue the chase were more than willing to follow Lind's command. The rest of the posse, who were more interested in going home, were reminded of why they'd agreed to come along with Lind in the first place.

Every one of the lawmen got his horse running toward the rider with the gun until the ground rumbled with a sound similar to a stampede.

Seeing what had been unleashed, the rider pointed his horse in the opposite direction and dug his heels into the animal's sides. That sent a wave of excitement through the younger lawmen, which turned the pursuit into a race to see who could nab the rider first.

"What the hell's going on out there?" Dell asked in a delirious voice that was becoming more slurred the longer he was forced to stay upright.

Clint lowered his spyglass and grinned. "Matt's doing one hell of a good job, that's what's going on."

"Sounds more like he's stirred up a goddamn riot."

"Exactly."

Clint watched for a few more seconds, until he was satisfied that most, if not all, of the posse members were chasing after Matt. Once the path back into Lohrens had been cleared, Clint flicked his reins so Eclipse could take a straight run into town.

"All right," Clint said. "Let's make sure the marshal has a nice little gift waiting for him when he gets back."

THIRTY-SIX

"Did you get Dell to a doctor?" Matt asked. "Or did you just drop the whining bastard off somewhere?"

Clint pulled back on his reins and took a moment to catch his breath. "As inviting as that second choice was, I followed up on the first."

"Oh well."

"Don't be too disappointed, though. I made sure the doctor knew who he was getting and why he should hand him over to the marshal at his first chance. Before I left, the doctor almost had Dell tied up even tighter than we did."

Matt chuckled and ran his fingers through his hair. "Damn. I almost feel sorry for poor Dell."

"Almost, huh?"

"Yeah, but not quite."

"Did the marshal or any of his men get any lucky shots in?"

"I didn't even see the marshal or any of his men. Still, I don't think we should press our luck by staying anywhere in the vicinity of Lohrens for a while. My business is done there, but I wish we could see the looks on some of those people's faces when they get word about what happens to Ben Jarrett after we get ahold of him."

"So you're still going after him?" Clint asked.

There was no mistaking the intensity in Matt's eyes as he replied, "I won't rest until he's taken care of. Even if he never came after me for that money I took, I would've gone after him sooner rather than later."

"So you really took all that money from Ben Jarrett's pockets?"

Although Matt had been intense before, some of his fire dimmed a bit and was replaced by a mischievous glint as he said, "Yeah. Every last penny of it."

"Do you know where it came from?"

"I doubt even he knows. It was pulled together from so many robberies, but a good chunk of it came from when they cleaned out the coffers of a railroad tycoon in Sacramento."

"You mean Harrold Winstrom?" Clint asked.

"You know him?"

"I read about him in the papers. It said he was supposed to have extorted money from all of his investors to pay for a new line running all the way to the Badlands. Turns out he just pocketed the money and tried to make a run into Canada."

Matt nodded like a proud poppa watching his child win a footrace. "That's the one. It was the perfect job, too. He stole all that money from folks who trusted him, so he couldn't just go to the law when the money was stolen from him. I bet he didn't even want it showing up in the newspaper."

"You really do strike down that whole honor among thieves idea."

"There ain't no honor where thieves are concerned," Matt said quietly. "Leastways, not among the thieves I've ever met. One thing I can say for certain is that Ben Jarrett don't even know what honor means."

Both men were riding at a steady pace, allowing the horses to catch their breath while still covering some ground. They were headed south, but hadn't exactly pinned down where they would wind up. For the moment, Clint was enjoying the calm after the storm as the sun worked its way to the horizon and bathed the land in a warm, purple glow.

"Speaking of Jarrett," Clint said, "do you know where we might be able to find him again?"

Letting his eyes wander in the same leisurely fashion as his horse's, Matt replied, "Not as such. I didn't ride with him for more than a few months, or maybe pushing close to a year, but he's not the sort to tip his hand to anyone. All I know for certain is that he'll be coming after me."

Clint nodded and shifted his eyes toward Matt so he could see the other man's reaction when he told him, "I do have an idea about that."

"And why do I have the feeling that the idea involves one of us dangling on a hook like a worm?"

Although he didn't want to confirm that suspicion right away, Clint had to admit that Matt was thinking along the right lines.

"It's all right, Adams," Matt said. "That's the same idea I had. Besides, putting me out there for Ben to find is a hell of a lot easier than trying to track him down."

"I'll do my best to make sure Ben doesn't get a clean shot at you."

"No need for the sweet talk. A man shouldn't make promises he can't keep."

"Don't worry," Clint said. "This is a promise I know I can keep."

THIRTY-SEVEN

Considering they had a gang of killers after them, Clint and Matt had a relatively easy ride farther into Wyoming. The air grew crisper and colder as the hours wore on, forcing them to pull on a few more layers to protect themselves from the elements. The cold also made every last sound crackle through the air and catch their attention like pebbles rattling on a tin roof.

Clint could never quite figure out why things sounded louder in the cold. They just did. Rather than try to figure out how nature's little oddities worked, Clint leaned back in his saddle and reaped the rewards of being able to hear anything bigger than a jackrabbit running his way.

Neither man allowed himself to relax fully, however, since even the coldest air wouldn't allow them to hear a rifleman sighting in on them. They kept their eyes open and stuck to trails that cut across wide stretches of equally open land. There wasn't much more for them to do beyond that. Everything else would boil down to keeping their senses sharp and their instincts sharper.

After riding for two days, neither Clint nor Matt had seen more than a glimpse of Ben Jarrett or any other men who might have been riding with Jarrett. Those glimpses had come in dribs and drabs, ranging from a fleeting bit of motion miles away to seeing a couple of men on horseback perched upon a ridge.

Clint and Matt had taken turns trying to get a closer look at these riders, but had never been able to find any of them. That only served to make Clint certain that they were either Jarrett's scouts or Jarrett himself looking in on them from afar.

Although Matt's good humor only grew better as they drew closer to their destination, Clint wasn't so quick to follow suit. When they finally reached the little town of Saddlewood, Clint raised his spyglass and took in the surrounding area through the polished lenses.

Saddlewood was a small place that basically consisted of one street and a few buildings scattered away from the two rows facing the street. Since it was situated in the middle of a flat piece of ground stretching for miles in every direction, the town wasn't exactly in danger of being taken by surprise.

"You sure about coming here?" Clint asked.

"Definitely. It's one of the main reasons I stopped stealing money and started handing it over."

"Would Ben know about this reason of yours?"

"Yep. And he would have made his way here one way or another. I'd much rather be here than let him have free rein."

Clint lowered the spyglass and tucked it back into his saddlebag. "Looks like we're on our own for now, but it wouldn't be hard for Ben to figure out we're here."

"It wouldn't have been hard to track us even if he hadn't been keeping an eye on us the whole time. Besides," Matt added while showing Clint a wry smirk, "isn't it the plan for him to know right where he can get to me?"

"You're right. Ride on ahead and I'll hang back here for a while so I don't get in the way of Ben's sights." Clint held onto his stony expression for a few seconds before letting out a short laugh. "So what brings you to this place anyway?" he asked. "Are you looking to hand out some more of that money?"

"There isn't much more of it left," Matt replied as he dug into one of his pockets. "But I figure you should have most of what there is."

Clint looked down at the hand the outlaw was extending and saw a fat wad of money in it that was close in size to the other ones he'd handed out. "What's this for?"

"Consider it a way of paying you back for the time you've spent helping me out."

"I didn't have any plans anyway."

"Then consider it payment for putting your neck on the line," Matt said with exasperation. "Just take the damn money."

Clint shook his head. "Keep it. I won't tell you again."

Matt grumbled to himself and stuffed the money back into his pocket. "I've run into plenty of firsts over the last few months and this is another one."

"Don't you have anyone else on your list who could use it?"

"There's more folks on that list than there's money in anyone's pockets, but that ain't the point. After this stop here, there's only one more."

"Sounds like you've got everything pretty well figured."

Shrugging, Matt shifted his eyes to the small town. The longer Clint looked at Saddlewood, the less it looked like a town at all. In fact, it seemed more like a populated stretch of road that just happened to have a few buildings lined up on either side of it. A few folks could be seen moving along the street, but there were as many figures wandering back and forth between the houses scattered around the main street.

"Where does she live?" Clint asked.

Matt glanced over at him again, but this time there was a bit of surprise on his face. "How did you know there was a woman?"

"Because you were more eager to move along where there've been guns aimed at you. Looking that banker in the eyes seemed difficult, but this seems to take the cake. More often than not, a woman's the thing that'll wind a man up that tightly."

Raising a hand to point at the west half of the town, Matt extended a finger and said, "She lives right there."

Clint looked as if he knew the exact spot Matt was pointing to. Even though he only saw a few scattered houses, he knew that Matt knew precisely where he was headed. By the look on Matt's face, he might already be picturing his walk through the woman's door.

"Her name's Faith," Matt said.

"Well what are you waiting for?" Clint asked. "I'm not coming along with you on this one."

THIRTY-EIGHT

Matt rode into town, feeling Clint's eyes on his back every step of the way. Every so often, he would glance behind him to see if he could catch Clint in the act. Clint might not have been standing in the same spot as the last time Matt had checked, but he wasn't far away. Every time he was spotted, Clint tossed him a quick wave.

Although he knew a quick shot of whiskey would have helped in facing Faith again, Matt kept himself from steering toward the narrow little shack marked as the only saloon in Saddlewood. A meal would have killed some time, but that was just another way to put off what he needed to do.

Swallowing his reservations, Matt pointed his horse toward the house he'd pointed out to Clint and snapped the reins. It was a short ride to the house. So short, in fact, that Matt felt surprised when he arrived at Faith's doorstep.

Matt kicked around the idea of turning back and buying himself that shot of whiskey. Before he could do that, he saw the front door come open and a familiar face look outside.

Faith's eyes were a peculiar mix of young and old. There was always a spark in them that made her look much younger than her twenty-eight years. On the other hand, there was a sadness and weariness around their edges that should have only belonged in someone who'd seen more than a young woman had a right to see.

For the moment, her eyes were more surprised than anything else. Matt was very happy to see the rest of her as Faith stepped outside.

"Matt?" she asked breathlessly. "Is that you?"

He nodded. "Yes, Faith. It's me."

At first, she stayed in her spot. It wasn't as if she was refusing to take another step. It was more like she'd suddenly lost the strength to do so. Faith was a petite woman who didn't come close to filling out the doorway. She wore a simple yellow dress, decorated with little yellow bows along the sides. The bows were ripped or frayed farther down toward the bottom of her skirt, which didn't take away from her beauty in the least.

Matt found it difficult to move, also. It would have been easier for a man dying of thirst to tear himself away from a well. He found his eyes moving up and down along her body, taking in every last one of her curves. Matt's eyes lingered upon her soft hair, which fell over one shoulder in a long, light brown braid.

Suddenly, it seemed as though Faith was nervous in his presence. "Did you want to come inside?" she asked.

Matt caught himself staring at her and nodded sheepishly. "I'd like that very much." Once more, he looked over his shoulder at the open land behind him. Clint was still in the distance and seemed content to stay there.

Faith led the way into the small, one-room cabin. It was furnished with the necessities and had the kitchen in one corner, the bed in another corner and the remaining space divided between sitting areas and storage spots. The little table was already set with one plate and a small bowl.

"I was about to have something to eat," she said. "Would you like to join me?"

"Sure."

As he watched her bustle around to fix the additional place setting, Matt wondered if she was going to ask the one thing that she truly wanted to. He knew her well enough to know how hard it would be for her to do that after being surprised this way.

"I suppose you'd like to know why I'm here," Matt said so she wouldn't have to.

"Yes. I was wondering about that."

"I know you probably don't even know why I left."

"You left because the law was after you," Faith said simply. "And I think there were some men looking to get the price that was on your head." Turning around with the freshly prepared plate and bowl in her hands, she asked, "Or is that reward still being offered?"

"Why?" Matt asked as he struggled not to show how surprised he was. "Were you thinking of cashing in?"

Smiling as she sat down, Faith picked up a spoon and tasted some of the soup in her bowl. "You know better than that."

"I guess I'm just surprised by how much you know."

"We were almost married, Matt. How could you be surprised that I would know something like that?" When she spoke again, there was a bit more of an edge in her tone. "Wait a moment, I know. You're surprised because you never told me and you never intended on telling me."

"I never meant to cause you any harm," Matt told her. "That's why I left. In fact, I stayed around you too long as it was."

Faith's eyes snapped up to look Matt in the face. There was an anger there that physically hurt Matt to see. "Don't ever say that! I wanted to be with you for good. That's why I agreed to be your wife. Then you pick up and leave in the middle of the night." Shaking her head, Faith poked at the soup again even though it was plain to see she was no longer hungry. "I waited all this time for you."

"You shouldn't have done that."

"It's not like there was a choice. Maybe you can snuff out what you feel, but I can't. I had to wait for you because . . . because I couldn't bear the thought that you could just leave and never come back."

"But I did come back."

"It's been two years, Matt! Two years and no word from you other than what I could remember you telling me before you left. That's all I had to keep me going."

"I figured you'd find someone else," Matt said. "Someone worth your time instead of a criminal like me."

Faith reached across the table and ran her hand along Matt's face. "Whatever you did before, I don't care. You're a good man. I would have liked a chance to make you better."

"You already did that," Matt told her as he placed his hand on top of hers. "Thinking about you is the one thing that made me decide to try and make up for what I done once they let me out of that cage."

"What are you talking about?"

"I was running from the law when I left you," Matt said. "The law and Lord only knows how many others who'd closed in on me because I'd stayed put in one spot for too long. No matter how much I wanted to stay, I just couldn't. I thought if I'd told you about it all, you'd just want to come with me."

"You're right," Faith said.

"And that would have kept you in danger when all I wanted was to keep you out of it. I handed myself over to the law because I thought I'd have a better chance with them than with some other folks who were out for my hide. I should've hung, but I found a way out instead. I tunneled out like a rat before the judge could send me to the noose.

"All that time, I swore I'd find some way to set a few things straight. I couldn't put everything right, because I'd broken just too many things for any man to fix. So I picked out a few that stuck out the most in my head and that were still somewhere I could get to again. I got some money and paid those good folks back the only way I could."

Faith shook her head and kept rubbing his cheek. "Will you stay with me now?"

Reluctantly, Matt replied, "Not for long. I just had to come here to make certain you weren't put in any more danger. You may even have to leave this place to stay safe."

"I can leave whenever you want, so long as you'll come with me."

Matt started to shake his head, but felt Faith's soft hand over his mouth before he could speak.

"Before you refuse, at least give me a chance to change your mind."

Her other hand was drifting to the ribbons that fastened the front of her blouse tightly against her breasts.

THIRTY-NINE

Matt tried to resist when he first felt her touch and knew she was standing up to move around the table and be closer to him. As much as his heart and body wanted to get up and wrap her up in his arms, his brain was protesting enough to keep his backside in that chair.

He hadn't ridden all this way to kiss Faith or even run his hands along her body.

Even though Matt had thought about those things ever since he'd landed in that dirty jail cell, he knew better than to let his guard down as much as he would need to in order to give in to her. For every one of his muscles that stayed still, there was another that flexed to get him up and off his chair.

"I can't do this," Matt whispered. "Not right now."

"What other time is there?" Faith asked.

Matt didn't have an answer to that. Before he could give it too much thought, he felt Faith's lips pressing against his cheek. After that, there wasn't anything strong enough to hold him back.

Getting up from his chair so quickly that he knocked it over, Matt swept Faith into his arms and kissed her the way he'd wanted to kiss her for years. Their lips met with a fire that had built up that whole time and was even more intense since Faith was burning with a fire of her own.

When Matt moved his lips close to her neck, Faith leaned back and let out a grateful sigh. She moaned softly as Matt kissed the smooth skin of her shoulders, and trembled when she felt him start to pull down the top of her blouse. A few of the buttons held up, but she wriggled so Matt could get his fingers under them and force them open.

"Oh God," she said as she worked to unfasten Matt's belt and get his jeans down. "I've waited so long."

But Matt was beyond words. He was too worked up to even think of what he could say, so he let his actions speak for him. Reaching around behind her, he placed his hands upon her firm buttocks and lifted her off her feet. He set her down on the edge of the table and lowered his mouth to her exposed breasts.

As soon as Faith felt the table under her, she reached behind her to sweep away all the plates, cups and utensils that had been set out. Even though a few things remained upon the table, there was enough space for her to scoot back and pull Matt closer.

Faith's legs wrapped around Matt's waist, and he slid one hand under her skirt to feel the smooth contour of her thigh. As his hand moved farther up her leg, he could feel his penis becoming rigid with anticipation. The next thing he felt was Faith's hand slipping between his legs so she could stroke him until he was almost painfully hard.

"Don't make me wait any longer," she pleaded.

Matt pulled her skirts all the way up so they were gathered around her waist. From there, he pulled off her panties so urgently that they ripped in his hand. Faith tensed at the sound of the tearing material and leaned back so she was supporting herself with both arms against the table.

Before Matt could get his hand between her legs to rub her in the way he knew she liked, he felt her hand guiding him into her. Matt felt her warm wetness immediately and he glided into her with ease. At first, she spread her legs even wider. Once he was buried inside of her, though, Faith wrapped her legs around him again and held on tightly.

Matt took his time for the first few thrusts. He savored the feel of being inside of her as if it was a dream. Unable to hold back any longer, he grabbed onto her hips and pumped into her with building force.

Faith leaned back and grunted as she took in every last inch of him. Propping herself up on one arm, she reached out to run a hand along his chest and look him in the eyes as he pounded into her again and again. Her face was intense, and whenever he began to slow down, Faith pumped her hips against him to urge him back into motion.

Before too much longer, Faith lost the strength to keep herself propped up. She leaned back on the table and grabbed hold of the edges as Matt continued to pump in and out between her legs.

Seeing the sight of her laying down with her hair splayed out and her eyes fixed upon him made Matt slow down again. He eased all the way inside of her and stayed there as the roar in his head died down again. He wanted the moment to last. He knew it couldn't last forever, but he didn't want it to be over just yet.

Matt slid one hand up and down along her thigh and used the other to move aside the material of her open blouse. Faith's breasts were small and pert, but fit inside his cupped hand. He teased her nipples and savored the feel of the smooth skin against his palm while slowly easing in and out of her.

Savoring a moment of her own, Faith smiled and wriggled slowly under Matt's wandering hands. She closed her eyes and arched her back as her climax worked its way up from the depths of her body. When she tightened her legs around him and pumped her hips again, Matt responded perfectly and plunged all the way inside her to push Faith over the edge into a trembling orgasm.

As she shuddered and groaned in the rip of her own pleasure, Matt built up another head of steam as he thrust

in and out, faster and faster. This time, he wasn't holding
back. He couldn't have held back if his life depended on it.
He'd waited too long and dreamt about this moment too
many times to stave it off for one more second.

A few more thrusts and Matt felt better than he had for
years. He slid all the way inside of her and locked eyes
with Faith one more time. Both of them stared at each
other as their breath slowly came back into their lungs.
Even then, it was a little while before they could speak.

Even after all the times Matt had thought about what
this moment would be like, when it finally came, he didn't
seem prepared for it.

Even after all the times he'd imagined this reunion, it
had somehow wound up better than he could have hoped.

FORTY

Clint didn't like the way things were panning out.

Recognizing the look in Matt's eyes when he'd even started to discuss the woman he'd come to visit, Clint knew better than to try and pry him away from that house anytime soon. Still, Clint couldn't just sit by and do nothing when he saw the other riders closing in on Saddlewood from the northwest.

The first one had arrived a few minutes after Matt had gone into Faith's house. Clint hadn't thought too much of it, since there were bound to be a few others riding into Saddlewood for one reason or another. Normally, Clint wouldn't have even been too suspicious when the next rider arrived.

The third one in such a short amount of time, however, had been more than enough to get him nervous.

Clint had tried to get a good look at each rider through his spyglass, but couldn't see more than a portion of a face before the rider disappeared behind a building or simply moved too quickly for Clint to keep up. He didn't need to see much to know the riders weren't arriving in Saddlewood just to water their horses or get something to eat.

Dropping his spyglass into his saddlebag, Clint flicked his reins to get Eclipse moving into town. The Darley Arabian carried him quickly to the solitary street. Since he figured Ben or his men would have spotted him already, Clint wasn't too worried about staying out of sight.

When he felt the hairs raise along the back of his neck, Clint snapped his reins again so he could get to some cover before someone could take a shot at him from an unseen vantage point. Whether that was just a nervous reflex or a life-saving instinct, Clint would never know. He did know that he made it to the edge of the street without getting shot, and that was plenty good enough for him.

Since it was the only real street in town, the signs painted on the few storefronts didn't have need of much creativity. The Saddlewood General Store sat across from the Saddlewood Hotel and next to the Saddlewood Livery. Sure enough, the Saddlewood Saloon and Saddlewood Restaurant weren't too far away.

As much as he knew Eclipse would appreciate some fresh hay under his hooves and fresh greens in his belly, Clint tied the stallion to a post he could reach from any of the businesses rather than purchase a stall in the livery. Patting the Darley Arabian's nose as he walked away, Clint headed for the first place he figured he could find Ben Jarrett, or at least one of his men.

The Saddlewood Saloon was as fancy as its name. Not much bigger than any of the other storefronts, the saloon had a broken front door and a dirty rectangular window built into the wall facing the street. Clint tried to get a look through the window, but couldn't see much more than a few shapes inside thanks to the sun reflecting off the smeared glass.

Pushing open the door, Clint waited a moment before stepping inside. The only thing that came out to meet him was the slurred voices of a few drunks, so Clint walked into Saddlewood's only drinking establishment.

What little space there was inside the saloon was taken up by a bar made up of a series of planks laid out on top of some old crates and wobbly tables. Behind the bar, there was a crooked bookcase holding several bottles of liquor. None of those bottles was marked by a label, and every one of them looked as if it'd been used several times before.

"Looks like a big day for visitors," a man in his late forties said from behind the bar. "You with the others?"

Clint glanced to where the barkeep waved to and spotted Ben Jarrett standing with one other man at a post with a shelf nailed to it. Both men leaned against the post and watched Clint as if they were thinking of new ways to gut him.

"Yeah," Clint replied with a smile. "We're old friends."

Not knowing any better, the bartender slapped the top of the rickety bar and asked, "What can I get you to drink, sir?"

"I'll take a beer."

"Comin' right up."

True to his word, the barkeep ran to fill a mug with beer as Clint stood his ground and waited.

There were a few others in the saloon, but none of them seemed too interested in Clint, Ben or the other stranger once Clint's entrance was done. They got back to their own discussions and turned their backs to the unfamiliar faces.

"Here ya go," the bartender said as he set the full mug down.

Clint took the beer, paid the barkeep and started walking toward Ben's table without once taking his eyes off of the two outlaws. He didn't bother looking for holsters around the other two men's waists and subtly shifted his beer to his left hand so his right could remain empty and within easy reach of his Colt.

"Fancy meeting you here," Clint said as he approached what passed for a table, but was actually more of a tray nailed to a post. Putting his back to a wall and keeping the front door in sight, he asked, "Where are the others?"

"Why, Adams?" Ben asked. "Were you hoping for a party?"

"Of a sort."

"Then you're bound to get your wish if you keep within ten paces of Matt Fraley."

"You're going to an awful lot of trouble for one man,"

Clint said. "Besides that, Matt seems more interested in doing a few good deeds and settling down."

"Maybe, but he stole from me before settling."

"So steal some more."

The corner of Ben's eye twitched as he fought to put on a convincing smile. "That ain't the point, Adams, and you know it. I can't let it pass when someone steals from me. Not even if it's one goddamn penny."

Clint shrugged and sipped his beer. "Then it looks like we've got a problem."

When the saloon door swung open, the smile on Ben's face became genuine. "Not for much longer, we don't."

FORTY-ONE

Clint's gun hand flashed down to his holster quicker than anyone else in that saloon could see. When he brought up the modified Colt to aim it at Ben's chest, Clint didn't even spill a drop from the mug he held in his other hand.

"So," Clint said, "did you mention something about a party?"

Ben blinked and looked down at the Colt as if he couldn't believe what he was seeing. The man beside him looked just as surprised, but started moving for his own pistol anyway.

"Don't be a damn fool," Ben hissed as he slapped at his partner's gun arm.

The man took his hand away from his holster and did his best to look tough as he shifted his eyes back to Clint. So far, nobody else in the saloon had seen or heard enough to pull their uninterested glances away from the man still standing in the front doorway.

"Wait for us outside," Ben said to the man in the doorway. When he saw the confused look on the man's face, Ben added, "Now, I tell ya!"

That brought from the others inside the saloon a few more glances aimed at Ben's table. Watching as the locals looked away again and got right back to their conversations, Ben was even more surprised to find that Clint had already holstered his Colt and was drinking his beer without a care in the world.

"All right," Ben said. "Fine. I still don't see why you'd go out of your way to help a no-good asshole like Fraley."

Clint held his beer rather than try to set it on the already crowded little table nailed to the post. "He hasn't done much of anything wrong while I've been around."

"He's a thief. A killer. From what I've heard, he's just the sort of man you're known for hunting down or even killing."

"I don't kill without a reason," Clint said plainly. "And Matt hasn't given me a reason."

"And what happens when he does?" Ben asked smugly.

Without missing a beat, Clint replied, "Then I'll kill him, just like I'll kill you if you try to push this any further than it needs to go."

Gritting his teeth, Ben started to pick up a glass of whiskey and then slammed it down hard enough to crack the little table halfway from the nails holding it to the post. "What the hell did Matt do? Did he pay you? I'll pay you double if you just get on that horse of yours and find somewhere else to be that ain't here."

Seeing the man in the doorway start to walk forward, Ben stabbed a finger toward him and snapped, "Get the fuck out of here!"

Those words echoed through the little saloon and brought every conversation in the place to a halt. Ben pulled in a breath and grinned at the bartender. "Next round's on me," he said. "Sorry for the ruckus."

The few others inside the saloon raised their glasses and voiced a quick round of thanks as the bartender hurried to refill their glasses.

"You're making a big mistake siding with a man like Matt Fraley," Ben said. "Unless everything I've ever heard about you is wrong, you know that just as well as I do, Adams."

"Matt Fraley served his time in jail," Clint said. "He's

gone out of his way to set some folks back up on their feet and he's not shying away from the sins in his past. Whatever he did before, he's going a long way to try and make up for it."

"Ain't no man can make up for killing."

Clint's eyes bored straight through Ben when he replied, "You don't have to tell that to me. All a man can do is try his damndest to set things straight, and that's what Matt's doing."

Ben squinted at Clint as his face slowly twisted back into a questioning scowl. "You said Matt served his time in jail?"

"As far as I know," Clint said.

"Then you don't know much, because Matt broke out of jail so he could set out on this little string of errands he gave himself."

Now it was Clint's turn to study the other man. He even looked to the gunman standing beside Ben and couldn't find a definite hint of a bluff among them.

Ben nodded as he felt his words sink in deeper and deeper. "You didn't know that, did you? What did Matt say? Did he tell you he stood up and pleaded his case in front of a judge who proclaimed him an innocent man?"

Clint thought back to the conversations he'd had with Matt. Sometimes, he thought he recalled Matt mentioning serving time in prison. Other times, Clint wondered if he'd just put those pieces together in his own head. Either way, Clint got the sneaking suspicion that Matt had danced around the subject so perfectly that Clint assumed it was resolved.

"Not such a good fellow now, is he?" Ben asked. "Just wait until he shoots you in the back or steals from you. Then you'll be chomping at the bit to ride along with me and string that son of a bitch up by his guts."

"Whether he served his time in jail, broke out of it or sprouted wings and flew out doesn't matter to me," Clint said. "Matt will pay his dues and it won't be by your hand."

"It'll be by your hand, then?" Ben sneered. "What the hell makes you so goddamned high and mighty? Why shouldn't he be judged by those he wronged?"

Clint only leaned forward a little, but that was enough to make it so that Ben saw him and nobody else in the entire saloon. "Because," Clint said, "something tells me you've done enough in your life that you earned whatever Matt did to you."

The corner of Ben's mouth jumped, making it look as if he'd been caught on a fisherman's line. "Yeah?" he grumbled. "Well you had plenty of chances to walk away from this. Next time I see you, I'll be sending your brains out the back of your damn head."

Clint nodded slowly and took his time finishing his beer.

Ben gathered up his men and headed for the door.

FORTY-TWO

When Matt stepped out of Faith's house, he saw Clint leaning against a tree not too far away. Since most of Saddlewood was situated in open ground, the tree seemed as if it had been dropped there by a twister and just happened to take root.

"Watching over me, huh?" Matt asked.

Clint stayed where he was, so Ben was forced to walk all the way over to him. By the time Ben got to the tree, Clint was grinning from ear to ear.

"What's so funny, Adams?"

"You look like you got a bit more than you bargained for in there."

"Jesus, were you looking through the window?"

"Nope," Clint replied. "I just need to look at that grin on your face. Was she worth the ride into town?"

"Oh yeah."

"Good. Was she worth breaking out of jail?"

Matt thought that over for a second and nodded. "Yeah. She was."

"So where does this reckoning of yours end?" Clint asked. "After you hand out that money, were you planning on stealing some more from someone else?"

"What would be so wrong with that plan?"

"Should I say like starting a bigger fire than you're putting out or just point out that you're not exactly making up for being a thief by stealing?"

Matt chuckled and nodded. "You got me there, Adams. I was just interested in hearing how you'd answer that."

"You've got my answer," Clint said without so much as cracking a smile. "I'd like to hear yours because I'm not about to stand by and watch you start another war with some other outlaw."

"I don't know if you've ever been in the Army, but this is far from a war."

"Not according to Ben Jarrett. He intends on taking you out no matter how bloody it gets or how many others have to get hurt along the way."

"He's here?" Matt asked.

"He sure is."

"And he told you all of that?"

"Not in so many words, but he's not about to let you off easy now that you're so close. I've seen his intentions in his eyes. When he mentions you or that money you took, he looks more like a wolf than a man. He's out to kill you," Clint told him. "And he won't settle for anything else."

Matt's eyes drifted back toward Faith's house. He was walking away from that little house before he even managed to look back at Clint. Still walking through an open stretch between the house and Saddlewood's only street, Matt said, "I knew Ben would be following us here."

"So did I," Clint said with a short laugh. "I watched them follow us the whole way here, remember?"

"Yeah, I remember. You must think I'm crazy for leading them here, though."

"Not if Ben already knows about this woman."

"Faith."

Clint nodded and took note of the subtle change in Matt's face when he said her name. "Right. Faith. If Ben knows about Faith, this is probably the best place for us to be."

Matt nodded and let out a relieved breath.

"Still," Clint continued, "no matter how good your intentions are for this money you stole, I can't just let you keep on robbing from the bad and giving to the good. You're not Robin Hood, you know."

Squinting at Clint's reference, Matt shook his head and replied, "I can't stay here, either. After breaking out of jail, there's men after me."

"I doubt it's too bad. That is, unless someone's renewed the price on your head."

"That should happen as soon as someone in that jail realizes I'm gone, and Lord only knows when that'll be."

"It shouldn't be too much longer after I take you back there so you can serve out the rest of your time."

When Clint said that, he shifted his hand a bit closer to the Colt at his side. His eyes remained locked on Matt, waiting to catch any sign that the man might not like what he'd just heard.

But all Matt did was nod. He looked more tired than anything else. The most emotion he showed was when he shot a backward glance at Faith's house. "Say what you want, Adams, but you gotta admit I'm doing more good out here than swinging from the end of a noose."

"That depends on how this turns out. You may just get an innocent woman killed."

"Nobody's gonna lay a hand on Faith," Matt snarled.

"And nobody would have much reason to if you were still locked up in your cell."

Slowly, the fire faded from Matt's eyes and he nodded once more. "I guess you've got a point there."

"You know I do."

"And what do you intend to do about it?"

"I haven't quite decided yet," Clint replied. The truth of the matter was that Clint had been hoping to make a decision when he saw how Matt reacted to this very conversation. Unfortunately, Matt hadn't done anything to push Clint away from his original path.

"Tell you what, Adams," Matt said. "I don't blame you for wanting to wash your hands of this, so we can part ways and call it a day."

Slowly, Clint shook his head. "I can't do that. I came along this far to see to it that you didn't get anyone else hurt or try to pick up where you left off as far as what you were doing before going to jail."

"I'm not that man anymore, Adams. You may not have known me back then, but you've got to know I ain't a killer no more."

"I know, but you're a thief and you're a fugitive from the law. I may not wear a badge, but I can't just turn my back on something like this. Besides, Faith is still in danger of getting caught in a cross fire."

"Not if I take her away from this place, go somewhere quiet and never look back," Matt said hopefully.

Clint nodded toward the gunmen that were walking straight toward them. "Too late for that."

FORTY-THREE

Ben Jarrett was flanked on each side by another man. All three of them walked toward Clint and Matt with their hands resting on their holstered guns. Stopping just over ten paces away from them, Ben planted his feet and waited for his two partners to get situated on either side of him.

Matt did his best to keep from looking at Faith's house, but he did manage to position himself between her and the three gunmen.

Clint stepped away from Matt so the three gunmen wouldn't be able to watch him and Matt so easily. Also, Clint wasn't anxious to give Ben only one large target to fire at instead of two smaller ones.

"You had your chance to steer clear of this, Adams," Ben announced. "But there ain't no backing out now."

"I wasn't going anywhere," Clint replied.

"Good. That means you can bear witness to Matt handing back my money." As he said those words, Ben straightened up and puffed out his chest like an artist admiring his own masterpiece. His smugness only grew when the men on either side of him leaned forward in preparation of the moment they were told to draw their guns.

Matt watched Ben's display with interest. In fact, he watched as though he were sitting in a comfortable chair as a play unfolded before him. After a few quiet moments, Matt finally spoke up. "Fuck you," he said.

"What did you just say to me?" Ben asked.

"You heard me. The money's gone, and even if it wasn't, I wouldn't hand over a single dime."

Ben glanced back and forth at the two men beside him. Until now, Clint was content to watch the two men posture in front of one another and spew out their tough words. He only got worried when he saw Ben give his two partners a subtle nod and then tighten his grip on the handle of his gun.

If Clint had had any hope that Ben could be talked out of making a wrong move, he would have started talking. If Clint had thought there was any way of changing Ben's mind, he would have given it a try. Since he'd already tried his hand at those things, he figured the best he could do was stand by and try to keep the approaching storm from doing too much damage.

Apparently, Matt was a bit more hopeful than even Clint would have given him credit for.

"Money comes and goes, Ben," Matt said. "We both know that. I know I took away a whole lot of it from you, but no money's worth your life."

"It ain't my life on the line right now, asshole," Ben replied. "Besides that, I can't let it be known that someone can steal from me and keep breathing. Not even if it's you."

Matt might have gone on to try and keep Ben talking. He might have even tried to bargain his way out of the fight that he'd known was coming all this time. But it was too late for that. It was one time that Clint hated being right.

FORTY-FOUR

Ben Jarrett and the two men with him went for their guns at the same time.

Clint pulled the modified Colt from its holster before any of the three men made a move, but only got a shot off at one of them. That shot was slightly off its mark since all three of the gunmen were firing at him.

Spotting the motion of the men's eyes as they focused in on him, Clint threw himself to one side while pulling his trigger. Even though he'd been expecting to be fired upon, being the target of all three was enough to make him nervous. Pulling his trigger while diving to the left, Clint saw his bullet clip the closest of the three gunmen.

Another shot blasted through the air when Matt's pistol sent a round of hot lead screaming toward the gunman on Ben's left. Since Matt wasn't the target of the outlaws' first salvo, he kept his hand steady, held his ground and dropped the gunman with one shot.

Clint landed solidly on the ground and was able to break his fall with his free arm before knocking all the wind from his own lungs. His gun arm raised as if he was pointing at his target with his finger and then he pulled the trigger. The modified Colt bucked against Clint's palm and sent a shot through the closest gunman.

Danny's head snapped back and his eyes blinked once in surprise. A confused expression drifted onto his face as he dropped to his knees and fell forward. Blood from the fresh hole in his forehead soaked into the dirt.

Still aiming at Clint, Ben fired two more shots in quick succession.

The bullets punched into the ground near the spot where Clint had landed, forcing him to roll backward rather than return fire. Even though he didn't have his sights lined up, Clint squeezed off a round as soon as he could. He didn't hit Ben, but he was able to back the gunman a few paces away from him.

"Son of a bitch!" Ben shouted.

When Clint heard that, he expected another shot or two to follow it. Instead, he heard Ben's voice shouting even louder.

"Goddamn son of a bitch!" With that, Ben fired once more.

Although Clint reflexively pressed himself low to the ground, that shot didn't come anywhere near him. The next shot didn't even come close. Seeing that Ben wasn't even looking in his direction, Clint got to his feet and glanced in the direction he was firing.

Ben fired in the direction where Matt had been a few seconds ago. This time, however, Ben was shooting at empty air.

"Drop the gun, Ben," Clint said.

Where he'd been cocky before, Ben was now just confused and mad as hell. He held his gun out and looked around as if he was trying to figure out how he'd wound up with the weapon in his hand. "Where the hell is he?" Ben shouted. "He was just here!"

"I said drop the gun!" Clint demanded. "We'll figure the rest out later."

As the confusion faded from Ben's face, only the anger was left behind. As the seconds ticked by, Ben's lips curled back into a snarl and his knuckles turned white around the grip of his pistol. "You were in on this, Adams. You know where he went."

Clint couldn't see Matt anywhere within the edges of his vision, but he wasn't about to take his eyes off of Ben to be certain. "This ends here," Clint declared. "You either drop the gun and we'll find Matt or—"

But Clint didn't need to finish that sentence. Ben finished it for him when he let out a profane shout and swung his gun around to aim at Clint.

The modified Colt barked once more from Clint's hand. It spat a short burst of sparks and smoke while sending a single bullet through the air to punch a hole in Ben's heart.

Clint reloaded the Colt and surveyed the area. As his fingers replaced the spent casings with fresh rounds, he searched for any sign of Matt. By the time he snapped the cylinder shut, he was still coming up short.

The next place he looked was Faith's house. As soon as he saw the front door to the little house swinging halfway open, Clint knew there was something wrong. He broke into a run, but knew what he would find even before he got there.

FORTY-FIVE

Nothing.

When Clint stepped into Faith's house, that was what he found.

Even though the little place didn't look like it had been much to begin with, there had to have been more than what Clint found now. There was a table that looked as if it had been swept clear with a broom, a few overturned chairs, some things scattered in the kitchen and a bed without any sheets or blankets.

Clint didn't even bother asking if anyone was home. There was no place for anyone to hide. Walking through the little house, Clint found a chest with a few odd pieces of clothing in it and an old wardrobe that was open and in a state similar to the rest of the house. Letting out an exasperated breath, Clint headed for the front door.

That was when he saw the note.

Written on a piece of paper and hanging from a nail that had probably held up a picture frame not too long ago, the note bore only a few sentences written in a hasty scrawl:

*Went to Canada. If we cross paths again, I'll let you
take me back to jail. Thanks for the help.*

Matt

Oddly enough, those words and the abandoned house
were more than enough to set Clint's mind at ease.

If Matt had wanted to turn on Clint, he would have done
so when the lead was flying.

From what Clint had seen, Matt Fraley really wasn't
such a bad fellow any longer. Clint's instincts even told
him to believe that Matt had truly gone to Canada as the
note said.

If Matt had wanted to rattle the cages of any more
killers, he wouldn't have taken Faith along with him. And
since Faith was along for the ride, Clint figured she would
be all the outlaw needed to keep his nose clean and stay out
of sight.

There was still the matter of the last bit of money that
Matt had stolen, but Clint couldn't get himself to be too
upset about that. Even if the money had been stolen from
someone else's pockets, it was being put to good use.

It wasn't a perfect way to end his ride with Matt Fraley,
but it was good enough. And sometimes, that was as good
as any man could ask for.

Watch for

WAY WITH A GUN

310th novel in the exciting GUNSMITH series
from Jove

Coming in October!

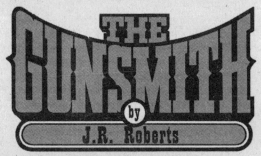